CW00382831

THE
BARLASTON
MURDERER

-

LESLIE GREEN

By Margaret Moxom

i

Copyright © 2021 by Margaret Moxom

Cover art copyright © 2021 by Margaret Moxom

No part of this book may be reproduced or transmitted in any form or by any means, electronic or mechanical, including photocopying, recording or by any information storage and retrieval system, without permission in writing from the author

Maggiemoxom@aol.com

Published by Amazon.co.uk 2021

Preface

This is the story of the brutal murder of Mrs Mary Maud Wiltshaw, on 16th July 1952, at her home - going by the name of 'Estoril' on Station Road, Barlaston. She was the wife of Mr Frederick Cuthbert Wiltshaw, the Governing Director and son of the founder of the pottery firm of Wiltshaw & Robinson, of Copeland Street, Stoke-on-Trent.

Leslie Green, aka Terrance or Terry, former chauffeur of the Wiltshaws, was hanged for the murder on 23 December 1952, but right up to the moment of the noose going around his neck, he denied carrying out the murder. I was intrigued by this - did he do the murder or not? Yes, you can say that he was an 'inadequate' character - a loser, a thief, and that drink played a part in the attack - he may have panicked and 'lost it' under the influence of alcohol – possibly. I was also intrigued by the fact that he presented himself to the police station, of his own accord. Now, why would he do that, if he had done the murder?

His memory loss could have been a way of avoiding a confession that he was involved in some way – maybe that he had been there but had not meant to kill his victim..... maybe that he was simply disingenuous, a liar and manipulative. It could be that Green was involved only in disposing of the jewellery and was scared of being implicated in the robbery and murder. The claim of memory loss and lack of a confession do not imply anything certain apart from giving the uncertainty as to whether he was guilty of murder or not.

i

I began to investigate anything on him, but there is nothing much I have been able to find on his background, his family, his youth, where he actually lived or even army service, apart from his convictions. Family heritage sites are not available to view for 100 years and, unfortunately, the records for 1921 are too early – Leslie Green was born in 1922. The army service number written on his wedding certificate in 1945, does not appear on war record searches either. He appears to be an enigma. Therefore, and I apologise in advance of you reading this book, but, even though the court case is factual, most of Green's background has been fabricated.

This book sets out the actual police investigations and trial - prosecution and defence cases - that led to his sentence of hanging. However, I wanted to give another possible side of the story that could conceivably have had a bearing on Leslie Green's state of mind at the time – a reason why he professed all along that he did not murder Mrs Wiltshaw and that he was elsewhere - a mind that, from his early childhood and mistreatment had manifested itself into loss of memory - when he experienced a sense of 'loss of time'. Please note that this is a completely fictitious notion and none of the history of Leslie Green before the trial, apart from his prosecutions, is factual.

What also came to light was the supposed 'deathbed' confession, many years afterwards, by an unknown person. Was this person involved in the murder and robbery? Could he have thrown a light on Green's involvement? Was Green protecting him? We will never know as this person died before the police decided to investigate.

You may find of interest the true life case that took place in America - "The Minds of Billy Milligan" by Daniel Keyes. Billy Milligan is charged with the rape of three women but had no memory of doing so. This was in 1977, so somewhat later than the Barlaston Murderer. Psychiatrists discovered that he had 24 persona and managed to bring him together somewhat to the extent that he could stand trial. It was the first case ever where someone was pronounced 'not' guilty' on the grounds of having Multi Personality Syndrome and was not sentenced to hang but to undergo further psychiatric treatment as a free man.

You may also find "Sybil" by Flora Rheta Schreiber, of interest. An earlier case. The psychiatrist Dr Wilbur was involved in both cases, acting as advisor for the Billy Milligan case. Dr Wilbur had spent years trying to bring Sybil's personalities together. Sybil was the first recognised case of Multi Personality Syndrome or DID. Dr Cornelia Wilbur's work was since discredited in the case of Sybil, but only after she had passed away and could not defend her work with Sybil.

Before the recognition of Multiple Personality Syndrome, doctors and police thought the people displaying this syndrome were either cleverly faking having other personalities as a means of evading the electric chair or hangman's noose for crimes they had committed or had other recognised mental health syndromes like psychopathic tendencies, neuroses, or borderline personality disorder.

Chapter 1

Alice Maud Mary Wiltshaw

It was 1950. Mr Wiltshaw was getting ready to go to his pottery firm of Wiltshaw & Robinson, Copeland Street, Stoke-on-Trent, where he was the Governing Director. His father had been the founder of this firm, long noted for its brightly coloured wares, usually marketed under the title of Carlton Ware and was much sought after by collectors and known and respect the world over. Mr Wiltshaw had taken over in the firm from his father Frederick Wiltshaw, the founder of Carlton Ware, when Frederick had died in an accident at Stoke Station.

Alice had prepared a cooked breakfast for her husband. He sat down at the kitchen table while Alice busied herself sorting out the cupboards and making a list of things she needed to buy.

"Will you be home early or will you be going to your club, dear."

"Oh, I think I'll go to the club, Alice. I should be home about twenty minutes past six or thereabouts."

"I need to go shopping, the cupboards seem pretty bare and I have seen a recipe in a magazine that I would like to try out. So can you get Leslie to drive back after he's dropped you off at the factory, then he can take me into Hanley, that's if you don't need him."

"Hm. I'll just look in my diary……. yes, that should be alright, I haven't got any meetings outside of the office today, just make sure he's back in time to pick me up."

"Of course dear."

"Leslie has been so helpful, carrying my packages and cleaning up, making the fire. He's a nice sort and everyone seems to like him. I think we made a good choice there."

"Yes, he smartens up quite well with the uniform we got made for him, and he's a good driver, doesn't speed and handles the car well."

"Yes, I've caught a glimpse of him coming to work in his old army clothes – he does look a sight. He keeps the chauffeur suit in the garage and changes there.

"Yes, I suppose I felt sorry for him with that hang-dog look of his and he was basically pleading for a job. Well, I was a bit bemused by him at first but, then I thought, well, he's ex-army, very polite and straight-backed – we need to do something to help our lads – they went through so much to keep our country free, having to come home with nothing much in the way of jobs they could do. I understand he's just been doing odd jobs here and there."

"And he's got a nice smile."

"Yes, he's pleasant, as you say. Plus he knows motorcars. He can take one apart and put it together again, just like a machine gun. He learnt that in the army, you know. I really don't know why none of the garages around her haven't taken him on. Anyway, it's time I was off, Leslie must be waiting outside for me."

Mr and Mrs Wiltshaw were the same age, 60, at the time, and had a good marriage with three daughters. Frederick Cuthbert Wiltshaw was tall, distinguished-looking with greying hair and thick horn-rimmed spectacles. He was a wealthy man, needless to say and their home, in Barlaston, Staffordshire, which they had called 'Estoril', after their various visits to Spain, was a veritable palace. It was a fourteen-roomed villa, standing on its own extensive grounds and surrounded on three sides by high hedges and beech trees. The house had good views across open farmland and the Trentham Park golf course where Wiltshaw was a member.

His wife, Alice Maud Mary Wiltshaw, was the daughter of the late Mr Tomkinson, Managing Clerk in a firm of Crewe solicitors. Alice was what some people would call, plump, but at 60, that was not thought anything out of the ordinary. She was always well dressed and manicured and had her hair done regularly.

....

It was Alice's birthday. Mr Wiltshaw gave Alice a card and said he would have something special for her on his return from work.

3

"Don't be late as the girls are coming over."
"I won't." and he gave his wife a peck on the cheek.

They had two maids, Florence Dorrell and Ada Barlow, who came every day about 8am. They had been sprucing the place up, ready for their guests in the evening. Ada had been helping Alice prepare the cake. Leslie had been cleaning windows and washing the car. The girls had gone by the time Mr Wiltshaw had arrived.

Alice was in the kitchen, finishing off making something special for her birthday tea and preparing the evening meal for her husband. There would be cake for when their daughters appeared. On display in the kitchen was a variety of Carlton ware items – the dinner service, bearing leaf patterns, the teapot and various serving dishes, displaying the same leaf pattern.

Mr Wiltshaw arrived home at his usual time. "Here, Alice, happy birthday. I've got a little something for you."

"Oh, you shouldn't have done, Fred."

"Oh, no shouldn't have done about it Alice. You deserve it. Here, let's go into the sitting room and you can unwrap it.

"But dinner will be spoilt."

"Oh, it can wait a few minutes. I just want to see your face light up."

They passed through the wide hallway leading out to the front door. There was a marble fireplace, in the hall, on the left, with doors to two other rooms. either side of the fireplace. There was a basket of cut logs, ready for the fire, a coal-scuttle and a vintage brass fire irons companion set of three tools on a turn-stand used for making up and tending to a fire – ornate tongs, a delicately designed shovel and a poker.

They went past the elegant oak winding staircase with marble treads and carved oak banisters. The floor of the hall was herringbone parquet, leading into the sumptuously decorated, high-ceilinged living room, a room you could describe of Dickensian character, with well stacked shelves, floor to ceiling, of books mainly. There were plant pots and vases of flowers. Some of the pots and vases were decorated with Greco/Roman figurines. There were also a few Carlton ware ornaments – a painted fruit bowl on the antique French, highly polished parquet top dining Table with 6 Chairs, all of which had curved, decorated legs. Hung from the high ceiling were a couple of chandeliers, sparkling - reflecting the remaining light. There were a couple of Carlton ware ashtrays dotted around – highly glazed leave shapes. The curtains around the high windows were brocade, draped midway over brocade and gold-tassled tie-backs attached with golden hooks. Lace curtains at the windows were scalloped at the lower end and the lace itself depicted countryside scenes. Looking around, Mrs Wiltshaw had displayed framed photos of their various trips abroad and various trinkets. Alice had travelled widely, being interested in languages and had, from time to time, employed foreign students, who came to this country to improve their English. The room was quite luxurious with a couple of Chesterfield leather suites and marble surround fireplace, Persian rugs and herringbone pattern wooden floors following on from the hallway.

There Mr Wiltshaw presented his wife with a carefully wrapped small package.

"Oh, what have you got me, Fred?"
"You'll just have to open it to see."

Alice carefully unwrapped the little box inside to reveal a most stunning diamond, ruby and emerald swivel ring.

"Oh, that's absolutely beautiful Fred." Mr Wiltshaw gave his wife a hug and peck on the lips. "Just to show how much you are loved, my sweet."

"Oh, sacre bleu, c'est absolutement fantastique. I shall wear that all the time." She tried it on and it fitted. Mr Wiltshaw knew it would fit as he had bought his wife, over the years, so many items of jewellery.

"Ok, time for your tea before it gets cold."
……………
It was the end of April 1951

"Oh, would it be alright for Leslie to take our grand-daughter, Alice and a friend on a day trip to Stockport to visit their former nanny. Say next weekend, when you won't be needing the car. Alice is so looking forward to going?" Mrs Wiltshaw asked her husband.

"Yes, I can't see any problem in that. It looks like it will be a nice day for them, according to the weather forecast. Maybe Alice might like to stay for a few days, then Leslie can pick them up, say on the Monday, after he's taken me to work."

"That sounds like a good idea. I'll ask Alice if her friend can stay too."

As it happened, Alice's parents did not want their daughter to stay overnight, so it was arranged for Leslie to take her back to her parents that same evening.

6

So, the two of them were placed in the car, along with a packed lunch. They were really excited at going, giggling as schoolgirls do.

On Alice's return. Mr and Mrs Wiltshaw asked about her stay. She was pleased to see her old nanny and had fun playing in the garden with her friend. Then, on the Sunday, after church, they went for a walk around Stockport. She had to admit Stockport was a bit grubby, with loads of factories in one area but they went to Lyme Park, where there were grand detached residences and cottages, quite picturesque, with views over to the Peak District. Mrs Wiltshaw asked if Leslie had found the place alright.

"Oh yes, he had no problem there. He was friendly but only spoke when we spoke to him."

"Quite right, Alice."

It was the next year now April 1952. Mr Wiltshaw came in to speak to his wife. He was looking quite gruff. "You know, Alice, I don't know if I'm being paranoid, but I'm going to keep a check on the mileage used on the car. I've a feeling our Leslie is taking the car, at the weekends, without my permission. Obviously I don't mind for the odd occasion, if he lets me know, but this seems to be a regular thing now. I think he's beginning to take advantage of us and that goes against the grain."

"That's a shame, as he's a nice lad. Can't you just warn him?"

"No, what I'll do is check on the movements of the car. It should always be in the garage of a weekend, if I'm not using it. If I see him, I'll say I need the car to go to some place or other. If it's not there, then I'm afraid he's had his cards marked."

So, it was May 4th, a Sunday. There was no car there. Mr Wiltshaw didn't have time on the Monday, with various meetings, to speak to Leslie, but on the 6th, he took Leslie to one side after Leslie had driven him back from the office.

"I apologise, Mr Wiltshaw, but I haven't taken the car."
"Well, if you haven't taken the car, you've given the keys to someone who has and that, in my eyes is stealing. I'm sorry, lad, but you had your chance and I won't be made a fool of. You've taken the car for your own purposes or, as you say, lent it to someone, too many times now, without asking, so that's the end of it. You can leave your uniform in the garage.

So, Leslie was out of a job once again.

Chapter 2

Terrance Leslie Green

They say that serial killers have two first names. Their mothers ensure it. They know that their little son is going to grow up to murder several innocents in about 26 years (give or take). It's called clairvoyance. Otherwise these women would have given their children only one first name, or perhaps 3. My mother gave me one name only, Leslie. That's the name I go by, to my friends – Leslie, but my uncle, mum's brother, wanted to call me Terrance. He is a nasty, obstinate, bully of a man, Anyway, he got it into his head that I should be Terrance, and no matter what my parents said, from the day I was born, to him, I would be Terrance. Christmas cards and birthday cards were always written out to

'Terrance'. So, basically, I had two first names, Terrance and Leslie.

I know of loads of people with two given names, but that doesn't make them serial killers. It's just a way of lessening the chance that someone with a similar sounding name might be confused with the killer. Take John Wilkes Booth – the assassin of President Abraham Lincoln. There's also John Thomas Straffen, who killed two young girls last summer, 1951. He was committed to Broadmoor Hospital. Or there was Robert Hicks Murray, a bigamist and mass murderer, who killed his children and one of his wives and attempted to murder his other wife. The police reckon he murdered at least seven other previous wives in 1912. Then, of course, there is Jack the Ripper, who has never been identified, but given this nickname.

But I'm not a serial killer - I'm not even a single killer. Yes, someone murdered my ex-boss, Mrs Wiltshaw, but it wasn't me. I wasn't even there. I walked into the police station as I knew the police wanted to ask me questions about the murder. I mean, I was definitely a suspect as I had worked for Mrs Wiltshaw, as her chauffeur, until she saw fit to let me go. Now, why would I walk, voluntarily, into a police station, if I had murdered poor Mrs Wiltshaw? That would be nonsensical. I would have vanished off the face of the earth, gone to some foreign clime, changed my name - just disappeared. Then I wouldn't have found myself in Longton police station being interrogated, a week after the murder.

Longton Police Station, Sutherland Road (from www.thepotteries.org)

While waiting to be interviewed I began to reminisce about my life and how I had got to this state of affairs. I had been born in 1922 so was 29 now, in this year, 1952. I would call myself stocky now, although I was a skinny little run-around as a child, probably because we didn't have much in the way of food. I never grew much more than 5ft 5in. I knew I had a boyish face, as so many people had told me – so, belying my 29 years. I also had a shock of dark hair. I had been in the army during World War II, and had emerged with a soldiery stance, meaning that, when I stood, it would be upright, back straight with feet slightly apart. Yes, the sergeant had drummed that into us, "Atten...shun! Stand upright, feet apart – you're in the army now. We don't want no slovenly people in the army". I was proud of that stance – it gave me a confident feeling, although I was feeling anything but confident now.

I grew up in Middleton, Leeds, in a rough area. My father had been quite a Victorian father, a bully, inclined to use his belt whenever I did anything that he thought disrespectful or out of order. I was a bit clumsy, especially in his presence, as he made me so nervous, which led to numerous beatings, especially when dad had had a skinful, which was a regular affair. If he couldn't get to me, he'd have a go at my mum and, being so small, I could do nothing to help her. Mum did all she could to protect me, even when she knew I was in the wrong. She called me Leslie but dad, whenever he was in a strop, would resort to calling me Terrance too, the same as my uncle did. It was as though my dad just wanted to disown me when I had done something wrong. The shout of 'Terrance' meant bad things were going to happen, followed by, "You're no kid of mine. I couldn't have a bairn of mine who was sich a barm pot."

Mum tried her best to retaliate, "Of course 'e's your kid. If you think I'd gone with someone else, well you can 'ave another think." But all she got was, "Shut your face." There was no good talking to him when he was in his cups. Of course, there were apologies the next day with promises he would never get drunk again, and hugs all round, but these were just unfulfilled promises. He'd get drunk because he didn't like his job – it didn't pay enough. Money was tight, and we couldn't afford much in the way of food, so quite regularly we'd go without lunch or tea, which also led to his moods and rages. Most times I just had the crumbs or gravy off dad's plate sometimes, so I was just scrag and bones.

He was nasty to me - take his drunken rages out on me and ma. We'd both get punched and beaten for the tiniest little mistake. I'd look at the big wheals coming up on my arms and legs – big red, swollen marks on my flesh, along with the bruises. I remembered one particular day, dad was at home – I suppose I must have been about five or six. He had asked me to get a bucket of coal from outside in the coal bunker. "What're yer doing theer? Faffing abart doing nowt and looking gormless. Yer neither use nor ornament, you. Get a bucket of coal for t'fire." I duly picked up the empty bucket by the fire and, putting a coat around me, went outside into the yard. The weather was bleak, with snow on the ground. I just got back through the back door, laden down with the heavy bucket, carrying it with two hands, using all of my strength to keep the bucket from scraping the floor, when all of a sudden I felt my feet go from underneath me and I slid across the floor on my backside, scattering the bucketful of coal all over the place. The floor was covered with coal dust which had floated up the kitchen table and chair legs, where it clung menacingly black and shiny.

"Hell fire! - Terrance, my lad – you're gonna get a good braying for that, came the deafening shout straight into my face as I lay still prone on my back. The spittle flared from his gaping mouth, which I tried to wipe away, only managing to get coal dust all over my face.

Next I felt myself being dragged to my feet, my coat ripped off me and my trousers pulled down as I heard the whishing sound of dad's belt being dragged through the hooks on his trousers.

Mum was shouting, "Lay off him, pa. He couldn't 'elp it. 'Is shoes got wet outside int snow and codna grip floor, so 'e slaped (slipped) – that's all."

But mum got pushed roughly aside and I felt the first whiplash coming down hard on my bare backside. Whoosh, and again, whoosh and another whoosh.

I was crying with the pain. "That'll larn yer, Terrance. Let that be a lesson. Now you get cleaning this all up en stop yer wingeing. Yer ma's got enough to do without cleaning up after the likes of you."

Mum got me a bucket of hot water, a scrubbing brush and a mop and I set to work, still with tears rolling down my cheeks, and my backside stinging with the pain. I couldn't even rub the area as this seemed to make it hurt even more.

I was sent to bed with no tea. I was so hungry, I started biting my arm, bringing blood to the surface. The salt on my skin tasted good.

I was angry. I couldn't help it, and I was still angry the next morning. I went out into the yard and kicked a few things, throwing stones and bits of old brick that were lying around, at any birds that ventured into the yard.

Mother grabbed hold of me. "Pack it in, Leslie. You don't want your pa catching you again. Good job 'e's off to work." Then she knelt down beside me and gave me a hug. "Those fowl 'aven't done you no harm, now have they? Theer just looking for food to feed their families."

"But, I'm vexed ma. I couldn't 'elp it. 'E'd no right to hit me like that. 'E's allus gi'ing me a wackin'."

"I know love, but 'e gets like that sometimes, so it's best to stay clear, especially when 'e's 'ad a few."

"But 'e ordered me to get the coal, and it was too 'eavy and 'e knew it was, and, anyway, I wanted to 'elp you out."

"I know lad. You've a good heart. Just take it in your stride if you can. You can't do owt about it, being so young. Now then, so 'ush, and come inside and I'll make you a brew and see if I can put together a few scraps for you. 'Appen he wain't be so mardy when he comes yam the neet."

14

"But ma, why does 'e call me Terrance when 'e's angry wi' me? You allus call me Leslie."

"Ah, I suppose it's 'is way. We all do it. It's just a bit of emphasis to make you realise you've done sommit wrong. Terrance is the naughty you and Leslie, I reason, is a better you, although Leslie can be a tyke too. Just donna let anyone push you around, you're better'n that. My reasoning is rules are made to be brokken, so best not to get caught doing sommit wrong, if you can, then you wain't 'ave to pay consequences."

Ma made a lot of sense to me when I was growing up, but the thing was not to get caught, as she said, which I wasn't all that good at.

Chapter 3

Superintendent Lockley conducted the first interview. A police woman was also there, with a notepad, presumably to take shorthand notes.

What faced us appeared at first glance to be a run-of-the-mill lad, pleasant faced, and polite. He looked younger than his years. You could see he'd had a military background as he addressed us as 'sir'. He was quiet, calm, answering all the questions pleasantly.

"For the record, you are Leslie Green, currently residing at 16 Elmore Avenue, Blurton, Stoke-on-Trent, with your wife, Constance Green and your 6-year-old daughter, Gillian."

"Well, this is true, in part. I am separated from my wife, Constance. She still lives at 16 Elmore Avenue, Blurton, with our daughter, Gillian.

"So, where are you living at present".

"I have a place in Beeston Street, Longton, but have recently been staying at the Metropole Hotel in Leeds as I have been travelling back and forth to Leeds. I was brought up in Leeds. But, if you're going to Beeston Street, you'll find a few things that don't belong to me. You know I'm a petty thief, that's what I do when money is short. You'll find a leather wallet, a cheque-book, and a driving licence that I nicked from Harold Ratcliffe in Weston Coyney, plus a few other things as well, nicked while I was working for Mr Wiltshaw."

Getting further full address details from Green, Lockley called a halt to the interrogation, sending Green back to the cells.

Lockley left the interview room and ordered a search of Green's premises in Beeston Street. There they found incriminating evidence of stolen goods. They had found the leather wallet, the banker's cheque-book, and the driving licence, to the value of 24s, the property of Harold Ratcliffe, from Weston Coyney, Staffordshire, stolen on May 30, 1952 as well as other items.

Lockley returned to confront Green with these findings.

"Yes," I answered. I stole 'em. I'm a petty thief, which you know already. I already told you about 'em." (Somehow or other I heard a voice in my head. They weren't my own thoughts. It said 'These stupid coppers. They don't know their arse from their elbow. I mean, how many times have you got to repeat yourself?) I didn't know where this voice had come from. I realised I must look annoyed as my normal pleasant smile had gone to be replaced by a grimace). I made myself smile again.

"Is there anything else you wish to own up to before I charge you?" I thought to myself that I might as well own up to everything I could remember that I'd nicked in the last year or so. Better be hung for a sheep as a lamb. I'd probably have to go back inside, but at least I'll be warm and be fed. "Ok, sir, I was just thinking. From what I can remember, there was a dress-shirt, a copper job, a small brass ornament - worth together, I suppose, about £2.15s. These I stole from Mr Wiltshaw sometime between January 1951 and July this year – little bits here and there, so's he wouldn't notice."

"So, you will be charged with larceny. Before that, as you know we are investigating the horrific murder of Mrs Wiltshaw, owner of the premises going by the name of 'Estoril' on Station Road, Barlaston. Mrs Wiltshaw was brutally murdered on 16th July this year, and we are investigating all persons connected with the house or were in the neighbourhood on that day.

We have been trying to locate you, having already made extensive interviews of persons who had been in the area. We have interviewed the two servants, Florence Dorrell and Ada Barlow. They also had a gardener and chauffeur, Roy Shenton, who had only been with them a short time. We have also interviewed Mr Challinor, who worked there with his assistant, Mr Brooks, and who rents the kitchen garden, orchard and paddock from Mr and Mrs Wiltshaw. There was also a jobbing gardener, a Mr Watkins, who worked for Mrs Wiltshaw at one time. He has a strong alibi too. However, you have finally attended here, of your own free will."

"Yes, sir, as soon as I 'eard that you wanted to see me, I came. I'm sorry, but I've been in Leeds and only just got back. I found out from t'papers you wanted to speak to me. I will try to 'elp you as much as I can in your investigations, but, as you probably know, I was dismissed by the Wiltshaws a little while ago, and I 'aven't been anywhere near the place since."

"We understand you had been employed as a chauffeur to Mrs Wiltshaw."

"Yes, I worked for Mrs and Mrs Wiltshaw from 22nd October 1950. My job was to drive Mrs Wiltshaw but also had to clean the fire grates and fill the bin with logs. I was also asked to clean the winders upstairs and darn (down)."

"So, you knew the building well?"

"As likes as mebbee, sir.

I presume you mean you had a good working knowledge of the layout of the building. Just answer yes or no?"

"Yes, sir."

The contents of the bag I had with me were emptied onto the table and the sergeant asked the secretary to take note that there were a pair of trainers, with a horizontal pattern on the sole.

"Where did you obtain these trainers, Mr Green?"

"They come from Majorca. A friend got 'em me."

"So, we can assume that these are probably the only pair of their kind in North Staffordshire at the present time?"

"'Appen as not, I suppose…. but nooo… if I've got a pair, it doesn't mean to say that no-one else 'as. The tyke (man) who got 'em, could 'ave bought loads over and flogged 'em arand t'neighbour'ood."

"Yes, quite." Lockley said gruffly, then checked over to see that the secretary had noted that.

"So, Mr Green, we need to have you checked over by our police physician, so if you follow me, we will take you to his office."

I followed and was asked to take my shirt off. The doctor examined me and made notes. He seemed very interested in a few scratches and cuts I had.

I was then returned to the interrogation room.

"Mr Green, following the inspection by our physician and the trainers you had in your possession, we have reason to believe you may have been involved in the murder of Mrs Alice Maud Wiltshaw. We will therefore be holding you, awaiting further investigation. I am arresting you at the moment for petty larceny. As to being a suspect in the murder of Mrs Alice Maud Wiltshaw, we will be investigating further. You do not have to say anything, but it may harm your defence if you do not mention, when questioned, something which you later rely on in court. Anything you do say may be given in evidence. Do you understand?"

"I did not commit the murder and I was nowheer near the property ont' date of murder."

"That is duly noted," and as he put handcuffs on me, continued, "but for the time-being you will be escorted to our holding cell."

"Just before we go, can you tell me if there's a young Irish lady darnsteers (downstairs) waiting for me? She's called Nora Lammey. I'd telephoned 'er to say I was coming 'ere. I would just like to say that Nora had nowt to do with this. She's my girlfriend, and I don't want 'er involved in any way. Don't take any notice if Nora has told you I go by a different name. I told her the first name that came into my head. She's not in it. I'm in this alone and fra what I can see, I've got that much chance" – making a circle with my finger and thumb.

"We will check," Millen answered, "but anyone having anything to do with you will be interviewed."

I wasn't happy about that but had to accept it.

Chief Superintendent Tom Lockley, head of Staffordshire C.I.D gave a report to the journalists gathered around the station. "I saw Green at 6pm yesterday and, as a result of what he told me, I later charged him with petty larceny, a theft to which he had already owned up to. Superintendent W Crook has asked for a remand in custody until next Wednesday. Further inquiries have to be made and we considered the remand was necessary. Green has also added that he did not wish to apply for legal aid."

Someone shouted out, "Have you got the Barlaston murderer?"

"This particular charge is of larceny and is no way related to the murder." Lockley then re-entered the police station.

Chapter 4

Before Leslie Green had presented himself to Longton Police station, on Wednesday, 23rd July, the police had been busy, and had set up an investigation team at Stone Police Station. Extensive Road blocks had been set up within the hour, stopping all traffic north and southbound. Drivers and their passengers were questioned and mobile police made random stops throughout the county. Also extensive road blocks were set up in Gaol Square, Stafford and at Newcastle-under-Lyme where all north and southbound traffic was stopped.

The general background given to the team was that on the late afternoon of 16th July, Mrs Wiltshaw was violently murdered at her home, which went by the name of Estoril, situated in Barlaston, Staffordshire. Lockley was saying, "He's still out there – somebody, somewhere knows something – question everyone in spitting distance of the scene."

The first person they interviewed was Mr Wiltshaw himself, as many police murder investigations had found that the husband was to blame. However, his alibi was sound and he was immediately dismissed as a suspect. His routine was to leave work at 5.30pm then go to his club where he would play a round of cards, then make his way home.

Mr Frederick Cuthbert Wiltshaw, aged 62, was the Governing Director and son of the founder of the pottery firm of Wiltshaw & Robinson, of Copeland Street, Stoke-on-Trent.

His wife, Alice Maud Mary Wiltshaw, was the same age and was the daughter of the late Mr Tomkinson, Managing Clerk in a firm of Crewe solicitors.

When interviewed, Mr Wiltshaw said of his wife, "Alice had travelled widely, being interested in languages, We have..... or should I say, my poor wife Alice had, three daughters, all of whom had been married at Barlaston parish church, which my wife and I attended regularly."

He went on to say, "My wife lived a quiet life and did not go out much in the evenings, preferring to sit with me, reading or listening to the radio. Every so often we attended the theatre or a charity performance, and more often than not our pictures would appear in the Sentinel."

Asked about the number of servants employed at Estoril, Mr Wiltshaw replied, "We have two servants, Florence Dorrell and Ada Barlow, who arrive each morning at around 8 and leave around 5.15 in the afternoon. I also employed a gardener and chauffeur, Roy Shenton, but I recently dismissed him. He had only been with us for a short time, following the dismissal of his predecessor, Leslie Green, on 6 May this year. As the house has extensive grounds we thought it appropriate to rent out the kitchen garden, orchard and paddock to a Mr Challinor, who works there with his assistant, Mr Brooks."

"And, Mr Wiltshaw, would you say you were a creature of habit or would your work and other activities mean that you would arrive home at differing hours?"

"Oh, I would definitely say that I habitually stick to my routine. I knew that my wife would have a cooked meal waiting for me on my return. I often call in at the Golf Club at Trentham on my way home from work and arrive home at 6.30 in the evening.

"You say 'often', so this means, not necessarily every day?"

"Quite, but more often than not I would stop off there. If only I hadn't gone to the golf club that day, I would have been home in time to prevent my wife's murder." There he pulled out a handkerchief, and wiped his eyes.

"I loved my wife. She was everything to me and so beautiful in her youth, but years wear us all down, unfortunately. She was always immaculate in her dress and usually wore one or two pieces from the extensive collection of jewellery I bought her."

"And was this collection of jewellery kept in a safe in the house?"

"No, I'm afraid not. She kept the jewellery in a case in the top drawer of the dressing table in our bedroom. I suppose, in hindsight, I should have purchased a safe but I never dreamed something like this would happen. We both felt fairly secure as there is not much in the way of robbery or violence in Barlaston. It is a quaint little village where everyone knows their neighbours."

"Did anyone on your staff know where Mrs Wiltshaw kept her jewellery?"

"Well, I suppose the maids knew, but I do not see why anyone else would go rifling through her dressing table."

"I know this is distressing, Mr Wiltshaw, but could you tell me what you saw, when you returned home."

"Oh, it was just dreadful.... but I will do my best, if you will be patient with me. This has been a great shock to me, but yes, I remember the scene as clear as daylight. It is a scene I cannot wipe out from my memory, no matter how hard I try."

Mr Wiltshaw started to shake a little bit and his hand was trembling as he tapped the desk lightly.

"I have been suffering from nightmares. I have not been able to sleep."

"Please, Mr Wiltshaw, take your time, but we do need you to describe what you saw."

Mr Wiltshaw started to get a bit angry then and raised his voice. "You've all seen what happened yourselves. You police have been all over the murder scene. Why do you need to cause me more pain by describing it to you?"

"I understand your reluctance, Mr Wiltshaw, but we need to write up our reports."

"Alright, if you insist." Then, Mr Wiltshaw, lit up a cigarette, obviously to calm his nerves, and he was provided with an ash tray.

"I came home at around 6.20, coming in through the back door, which led to the scullery and on into the kitchen. I was expecting a cheerful 'hello' from my wife and I called out to her, but got no reply. It's then I saw, going into the kitchen, that all was in complete chaos, with pots and pans strewn everywhere and the potatoes being cooked for my dinner, spread over the kitchen floor. My first thought was that there had been an accident of some kind. I went on into the hall, calling my wife's name. It was there that I discovered the body of my wife, lying on the floor near to the front door, her head and face were a mass of wounds. I was going to kneel down to her but she was lying in a pool of blood. I could see that she was dead – no-one could have survived those horrific injuries. My next thought was to telephone my neighbour, Dr H J Browne and he hurried round. He examined the body and shook his head. There was no hope. I then rang the local Barlaston police and spoke to PC John Bigham, and about 20 minutes later, that's when the detective sergeant, Alf Robins, from Stone police station, arrived, with his superintendent William Crook and several other policemen."

"Yes, PC John Bigham telephoned the Stone police station. Did you see anything that may have been used in the attack?"

"Yes, our old fire poker was close by and some blocks of wood for the fire, oh, and a hammer."

"We noticed that the poker was bent. Can you confirm this poker was bent beforehand?"

"No, to my knowledge it was as straight as a die, but it was unusual, having a barb on the end."

"Thank you. What we need now is an account of all items of jewellery and any other items that are missing, if you could provide that as soon as possible please."

"What I did notice, in my stressed state, was that two rings that my wife usually wore on her fingers, were missing. She didn't normally take them off. It looked like the killer had wrenched them off her fingers as there was bruising. I want this blighter caught and I'm going to offer a reward for anyone giving the whereabouts of the jewellery." Mr Wiltshaw stated angrily.

I thanked Mr Wiltshaw for his account and said that we would do our utmost to apprehend the attacker and bring his wife's killer to justice. We checked the time Mr Wiltshaw had left the club, which confirmed his statement and Mr Wiltshaw was deemed no longer a suspect.

An hour after it was known that valuable jewellery had been stolen from the Wiltshaw home, the two daughter of Mrs Wiltshaw, one a doctor, were taken by Chief Detective-Superintendent Lockley to a firm of working jewellers in Birmingham, where a craftsman fashioned mock jewellery from their description of the missing pieces.

The mock jewellery was photographed and copies sent to all police forces in the country.

……………..

The next person to be interviewed was Dr H.J Browne. He gave a more detailed report of the wounds inflicted. "There were cuts to the dead woman's hands that indicated that she had put up a spirited defence before succumbing to a hail of blows. From the pooling and trail of blood leading from the kitchen to the hallway, my impression is that Mrs Wiltshaw had been knocked to the floor. Presumably, and I can only surmise, with the bloody hand marks on the hall walls, that Mrs Wiltshaw had actually managed to stand up, and get to the hallway, possibly while the murderer had gone upstairs to search for the jewels. I presume, hearing movement downstairs, brought the attacker back and, seeing her still alive, provoked another attack on her, with missiles being thrown at her of anything that came to hand, a vase, ornaments and lumps of wood for the fire, a walking stick and a large brass bowl. Mrs Wiltshaw tried to escape back towards the kitchen. There, collapsing on the floor, dying. The callous killer stabbed her through the head with the poker. He also stabbed her in the stomach a number of times."

Police Inspector Alf Robbins was asked for his report. He related the scene then added, "I went into the kitchen, where the assault had begun. There, on the floor, I spotted wet shoe prints, which were very clear and had a horizontal pattern across the sole. This was most unusual footwear and I reckoned straight away that the marks had been made by the person responsible for the murder.

27

I got something out of the garden to cover them up. Then our police dog found a pair of blood-stained chamois gloves in the rose garden. The left one had a cut in the thumb."

Superintendent Thomas Lockley then went to address the team, giving them an outline of the scene that presented to him on entering Estoril.

"In the kitchen, the floor appeared to have been recently cleaned and the table, which had bloodstains on it, was laid for a meal. Pieces of broken pottery lay alongside Mrs Wiltshaw's tortoiseshell spectacles and a saucepan handle and vegetables prepared for cooking were scattered about the floor. There were further bloodstains in the passage leading from the kitchen into the hall, and on the jamb of the communicating door were marks in blood that appeared to have been made by a gloved hand. In the hall, by the fireplace, were a hammer, an antique steel poker, about 3ft long, with a barb in the end and a piece of wood. The poker was bent, although the distraught Mr Wiltshaw was certain that it had not been bent when he went out that morning. A quantity of water had been spilled in the kitchen and there were several footprints, which Inspector Alf Robbins carefully protected. It looked like the murderer had trodden in earth in the garden which made prints in the kitchen, plus there were the same prints walked through the blood on the floor. In the drawing room, that day's Evening Sentinel lay open on a small table and a lady's handbag lay discharged on the floor. It contained a chequebook, some personal papers and keys."

Supt Lockley continued, "As you know, we've set up roadblocks, questioning drivers, passengers and passers-by. Checks have also been made at mental institutions, approved schools and Borstal institutions, checking for absconders. What has come out of that is that three women, living near the Wiltshaw's have given information about a young, fair-haired man they'd seen in the neighbourhood, just hours after the murder.   I want him apprehended and an identify parade held."

I was actually in that parade, with 11 other men, but two of the women were unable to pick out anyone they recognised and the third picked out another man before picking me.

Lockley wasn't happy about that, naturally, but it was before they knew I had been a chauffeur to the Wiltshaws and they were looking for a fair-haired man, and I was allowed to go. "So, they're still looking." I said to myself. "Shame about Mrs Wiltshaw. She was an old biddy, but no-one should be murdered in that way."

More information was coming in, so Lockley addressed the squad again, "We are anxious to interview a youth of between 16 and 20 years, who had been seen near the house earlier in the afternoon. He was reported to have been of average height and wearing grey clothing. I want you all to be on the look-out for him. We also believe that Mrs Wilshaw knew the intruder and it was someone who knew the household routine very well indeed. This, in turn, suggests that an ex-employee would be the right kind of candidate. There was a chauffeur employed until recently, who was dismissed, following the dismissal of the previous chauffeur, Leslie Green. We need to find this previous chauffeur and Leslie Green. I want posters put up and notices in all the newspapers for anyone knowing the whereabouts of these two people, and of course, the youth."

There was immediate chatter amongst the team and someone called out, "Looks like we know who we want. We'll get the b...... and we can have an early arrest."

Chapter 5

Meanwhile the body of Alice Wiltshaw was taken to the police mortuary to await a post-mortem by Professor J M Webster. He conducted the post-mortem the following day. He noted that she was a stout, elderly woman, 5ft 5½in in height. In life, she had suffered from a stiff right elbow joint, which would have rendered that limb ineffective either in defence or offence. "She has many grave injuries, from which a great deal of blood had been lost, including several stab wounds to the abdomen and right shoulder. The lower jaw was completely shattered and a large gaping wound extended from left of the bridge of the nose to the right ear. There are defensive wounds to the dead woman's ring finger that, in my opinion was definitely from the warding off of blows. The top of the skull had been beaten in and I thought that some of the wounds could have been caused by the steel poker found in the hall. Mrs Wiltshaw's blood was Group A, but there were other stains belonging to Group O, notably on a raincoat."

The inquest on Mrs Wiltshaw was formally opened at Stafford yesterday afternoon before Mr K T Braine-Hartnell, the Coroner, and was adjourned pending investigations by the police, to a date to be decided later.
....

As it happens the lead for the youth came to nothing. The lad had a sound alibi. All the staff were interviewed but nothing out of the ordinary discovered.

Lockley addressed the team again, "Searching the grounds, a police dog, named Rex, had been brought in and eventually discovered a pair of hogskin gloves that had been thrown into some bushes at the rear of the house – size 8½ and made by Dents. The gloves were rather grubby and on the left-hand thumb was a tear, about half an inch long, which looked as though it had only been done very recently as the material in the cut was clean. One glove had a pearl button attached at the wrist; this was missing from the other glove and was later found adjacent to Mrs Wiltshaw's body."

"Super" this was one of the team, "We've discovered that Mrs Wiltshaw received a telephone call at about 5.15 in the afternoon on the day she was murdered."

"So....," replied Supt. Lockley, "that narrows down the time of the murder considerably. We don't know how long she was on the telephone, say 10 minutes, so between 5.25 and 6.20, when Mr Wiltshaw arrived."

Speaking to his sergeant, Lockley put forward an idea that he had been mulling over. "I'm going to work on a hunch, just to test a theory. I'm going to go to Stafford and take the train back, just to see if the times match up."

So Lockley went to Stafford Station and caught the 5.10 train to Barlaston. Arriving at 5.40, he climbed over the fence and walked through the fields to the wicket gate behind Estoril. That walk had taken him seven minutes. So, he surmised, the walk back would take another seven minutes and he could catch the 6.05 train back to Stafford. That left a gap of eleven minutes at the Wiltshaw's house – would that be enough time for Green to enter, steal the jewels, be caught in the act and kill Mrs Wiltshaw? Maybe if he ran?

On returning to the police station, Lockley gave his result to the sergeant. "It's very tight, but he could have done it. I think we've broken Green's alibi!"

Lockley continued, "We have also received further information from Mr Wiltshaw. He has told us that his old RAF raincoat has been taken. We need to find that raincoat. I want inspections done on all the trains and buses leaving Barlaston that day – check the left-luggage offices.

Later that day, Cedric Wiltshaw handed to the police a list of items that he believed had been stolen by his wife's attacker. Altogether they numbered twenty-one items, which he estimated the total value as being £3,000.

Lockley told his team, "I am putting on the board a description of the jewellery. I want the team to check all pawn-brokers, so get them cracking on the phones."

The list that went on the board set out the 21 items stolen. Some of which were:

A lady's platinum and diamond wristlet watch, valued at £100
A diamond ruby and emerald swivel ring (£36)
A sapphire and diamond ring (£50)
A diamond baguette ring (300)
A platinum and diamond eternity ring (30)
An Emerald and diamond bracelet (£230)
A man's gold cigarette case
£20 in notes
A man's RAF raincoat.

At bit later on Lockley addressed what members of the team were there, which included PC Dobson from the Stone office. "There has also come in a report that a villager had also seen a man in grey running away from the back of the house towards the station. Dobson, I want you to check that out – get a statement."

"Sir," this was Dobson, "I've checked the whereabouts of the previous chauffeur, the one only there for a few weeks, and he has a tight alibi – he was working at the time, driving his new boss to Manchester. I've also checked on a chauffeur they had pre-war, a Mr Clare but his alibi checks out too."

"Right…. that means our prime suspect appears to be this 29-year-old Leslie Green, an ex-borstal boy. He had used Mr Wiltshaw's car without permission and had been dismissed for disobedience, just a few weeks before the murder. I want this man found."

……………..

Just after this, Leslie Green presented himself to Longton Police Station and had been interviewed.

Supt. Lockley had a quandary now, whether to call in Scotland Yard or not. He was a bit dubious about doing so, but the social standing of Mr Wiltshaw probably influenced him plus the fact that Green was staying in Leeds, meant that he could have hidden the jewels there or even have connections in Leeds for disposing of the jewels – so this took the investigation out of Staffordshire. The jewels could even, by now, be anywhere in the country or even overseas. It was really beyond his remit, although he was sure he had the killer. To take the investigation out of his hands would mean, obviously, that Longton police would not get the credit for getting the killer, but the picture was bigger than that. So, Supt Lockley decided to contact Scotland Yard.

Supt. Reg Spooner was summoned from London to assist, together with Detective Sergeant Millen.

Chapter 6

Supt Spooner and Detective Millen went in to interview Leslie Green at Longton Police Station.

Spooner said to him, "We propose to question you as to your knowledge of the matter at Barlaston and your movements on the day in question."

Green appeared unmoved and merely replied, "Alright".

I (Detective Sergeant Millen) remember thinking to myself that, faced with a murderer – a man you know in your bones is a killer – how does one begin an interrogation like that?

I took down his statement in longhand, part of which read:

"On Thursday, July 17th, I left the Metropole Hotel in Leeds at about 10.30am to go home for the weekend. I bought a paper and returned to the hotel at 11.30am. I had the Daily Express and read of the murder of Mrs Wiltshaw at Barlaston. As I was staying at the metropole in the name of Wiltshaw of Estoril, I went back to the hotel and told the receptionist it was a relative and I would have to go immediately. As I came out of the hotel, I met two chaps I knew, one called Lorenzo and the other Charles. I had first met Lorenzo at the Cameo Ballroom in Longton when I worked there in the evenings. They were supposed to meet me in Spinks's bar in Briggate near the station on the previous Monday evening. I had told them about a fortnight previously to get me two rings, an engagement ring and a wedding ring, as I wanted to give them to Nora (my girlfriend). I went to keep my appointment but they didn't come in. When I saw them on the 17th, I asked them if they had got my rings and Lorenzo said, 'Yes'. He gave me the two rings in little ring cases and I asked them if they had any money. Between them, they gave me £15."

I thought this a curious transaction, seeing that Lorenzo and Charles had just handed over two rings, for which they had received no money from Green.

Supt Spooner had then asked Green where Lorenzo and Charles got the rings from.

The statement went on to say "Lorenzo had asked if there was jewellery in the house, then asked him how to get into the house and I said that there were two doors, one at the front and one at the back. At no time did I agree with him to break into the house and I can't say who killed Mrs Wiltshaw. I have never discussed with anybody how to get into the house or about the fields at the back, nor about the land that is cut through from Broughton Crescent to the fields."

Afterwards, Supt Spooner and I went through the murder scene together, the bent poker and the two rings missing from Mrs Wiltshaw's hands. The killer had obviously worn gloves as there were no finger-prints, nor was there any sign of a break-in.

We were driven to Stone Police Station, with Green and his girlfriend, Nora Lammey, where we would base our investigations and carry out interviews, interrogating Green again.

. . . .

Getting back to Longton Police Station, the PC driving the car, spoke to Lockley. "He's a strange guy this Green. He acted as if this was all a bit of fun for him, like he was out on a day trip or something. He was even pointing out buildings and their history to the Super and Sergeant, He was so relaxed. I've never seen anything like that. Normally prisoners are edgy, stressed-like, keeping themselves to themselves, but this one gave me a bit of the creeps if you don't mind me saying."

"Not at all. I found him strange too. Yes, calm and collected, giving all the indications that he was innocent of any violent crime – quite a nice, gentle sort of person. But, then I'd catch a look in his eye as though we thought we were all a load of dimwits – a sort of a nasty look came over him and I could well believe he was the violent criminal we think he is."

"He's definitely two-faced, if you ask me."

"Well, it's out of our hands now. Scotland Yard can have him. They can have our findings, but you know what Scotland Yard's like, they'll have to do their own searches, ask the same questions as though we're a bunch of country bumpkins!"

"Wasting time, if you ask me." the PC replied.

"Shame we had to let the case go to Scotland Yard as we know we have the killer."

Chapter 7

Arriving at Stone Police Station, Supt. Reg Spooner called out to Alf Robbins, as he and I, Detective Sergeant Millen, entered the door with the prisoner in tow, "Robbie, he's got the shoes!" This obviously intended to convey to Alf Robbins that Green had in his belongings the shoes with the horizontal pattern across the sole, the same as the imprints made in the blood on the kitchen floor.

Courtesy of Stoke Sentinel

With Green in the cell, Supt Reg Spooner discussed the case with me and Alf Robbins. "I've got the report from the Longton police doctor. It states that Green has scrape abrasions on the front of the right wrist, now scabbed over, consistent with having been caused on or about 16th July. There was also a similar type of wound close to the ball of the right thumb and a small wound on the left thumb. That fits nicely with the gloves that were found in the garden. Unfortunately, as far as I see it at present, all of this could be entirely circumstantial as he says he got the cut elsewhere, but it's all coming into place, like a mosaic."

Supt Spooner and I, Detective Millen, intensively interrogated Nora Lammey that same day, 25th July. Supt Spooner discharged her late on in the evening. He advised the papers that no charge against her was being considered at present, but that she may be summoned to give evidence at any future court proceedings.

The Staffordshire Sentinel headline banner screamed:
'ACE SCOTLAND YARD MAN CALLED TO BARLASTON MURDER'.

The next day, Supt Spooner addressed his team, "As you know, I have been asked to head up this investigation, so everyone comes to me first. I want the team split into two, team one to do searches and team two to gather statements"….. Then after the teams were sorted, added, "OK, you've got your assignments. Let's turn over some stones and see what crawls out."

Spooner also organised an appeal to the Barlaston villagers. He requested that all residents in Barlaston were to report to the nearest police station. The villagers are asked to go to the police even if they had noticed nothing out of the ordinary.

Mr Wiltshaw had been cleared of the murder at Longton but Supt Spooner and I interviewed him again, at Stone. We reckoned that Mrs Wiltshaw must have been killed between 5.20pm when the household staff left and her husband's return. He had been playing bridge at the crucial time. He told us about the missing jewellery that was in a case, a gold cigarette-case and a wallet and purse from his wife's handbag, as well at the old RAF raincoat that had gone from the lobby."

"Could you identify the RAF raincoat?"

"Yes," he replied, "there were three spots where it had been burned with a cigarette." I filed this fact in my memory.

So, we had one little clue to start with …. Three cigarette burns on an old mac – a trivial detail, you might think, but we weren't going to dismiss it. It could be a vital lead, no matter how circumstantial at present. If we could just find that coat.

Alf answered, "If we could find that missing RAF raincoat. I've a suspicion there may be blood on it that matches Mrs Wiltshaw's blood."

"Also, I'm afraid, circumstantial. If it was Mr Wiltshaw's coat – there could have been blood on the coat beforehand. When we find it, and I'm sure we will, we will need to check the blood type, although most people come under just three blood types, so the jury would throw it out. If there is blood we have no proof how the blood might have got there – perhaps he had a nose-bleed and wiped his nose on the sleeve."

"Oh, I'm sure that wouldn't have happened." Replied Alf. Mr Wiltshaw is a gentleman and would have had a handkerchief. There's no way he'd wipe his nose on his sleeve than, excuse me for saying, pick his nose."

"I agree with you there, still, we have to find that raincoat and find what we find. Lockley at Longton has put out an all bulletins to find it. Anyway, I have been supplied with Green's record sheet." Here Spooner opened his suitcase to produce the report. "It says here that he has received various periods of imprisonment for theft, including three years in Borstal in November 1943 and a month for being in possession of two firearms without license." Looking further down the log, Spooner noticed something else, "Hmm, it seems that there is a report here from the Borstal institution stating that there was, in their words, 'A reasonable probability that Green will abstain from crime and lead a useful and industrious life' and he was recommended for discharge on 28 February 1945."

"I bet they say that for everyone – they just want them off their hands. I bet also Mr Wiltshaw wouldn't have employed him if he knew he had a criminal record."

"Quite." Reading further, Spooner read out the following: "It seems that Green had been a serving soldier since 1939, the start of the war, and would be returned direct to the army. Hmm, it seems he got married to a Constance Eunice Elizabeth Gunn on 18th May 1945 and the address given was 63 Harvey Road, Meir. He gave his father as Harry Henry Green, but he was noted as deceased."

"That seems a bit odd to me, Reg, going from the army to Borstal and then back to the army again. I'm sure something's wrong there. They must have got their dates muddled up or something. Miscreants in the army aren't sent to Borstal, they're normally put in the Glasshouse and, if they have been sentenced, they aren't allowed back in the army again."

Spooner immediately alerted the Leeds constabulary and ordered house searches of Green's remaining relatives still living there. Getting the Leeds force involved, an all-round search was ordered, visiting lodging houses and long-distance road transport garages in Leeds in an effort to trace Green's movements. Drivers of long-distance transport vehicles, travelling between the Potteries and Yorkshire were to be interviewed.

Earlier yesterday, Barlaston police constables discarded jackets, rolled up their sleeves and tucked trousers into socks before they scythed a large field behind Estoril, the home of Mrs Wiltshaw.

They made an unsuccessful search for the jewel case and items of blood-stained clothing, which the murderer might have discarded in his flight from the house.

The Advertiser headlines were:
'NIGHT POLICE SEARCH FOLLOWS BRUTAL BARLASTON MURDER'

PC Dobson and others from the Stone police force, including a PC Gregory, were out talking to locals from Barlaston.

The general feeling was that people were scared. This was a small, community and the savagery of Mrs Wiltshaw's killing had sent shock waves also across post-war Britain, where families still left their house door unlocked.

Many of Barlaston's 600 inhabitants were too scared to speak to strangers while others had pet dogs by their side for safety.

More than 600 people made statements to a team of detectives who flooded the area and even an appeal for witnesses was broadcast over the tannoy system at the Wedgwood pottery factory nearby.

A Mrs Cooke said, "He's a real nice feller. Always 'elpful. I can't believe 'e did such a nasty thing, no, you've got the wrong man."

They also went to Embrey's Bakers, where Green had worked before he went to work for Mr Wiltshaw. PC Dobson spoke to a Barbara Edwards, who was working in the office.

"He used to take deliveries of bread to the shops in Stoke. He seemed a nice guy. Of course, you wouldn't know, but I also worked at Wiltshaw and Robinsons and saw him a few times, driving Mr Wiltshaw there, and back home. I'd nip out for a quick cigarette with him. He was a bit of a laugh, just a normal run-of-the-mill guy, but kind and gentle-like, not rough like some of the lads. I would never have thought he would have done something like murder. He just wasn't the type."

A lady, about 60-years-old, by the name of Ada Pritchard, reported to the police, as requested to do so. Again, she didn't have any information of note but just to say she knew him and if they do hang Leslie Green, we will have hanged the wrong man.

The grand-daughter of Alice Wiltshaw came to the police station. She told us that Green had taken her and a friend, Barbara, one day on a day trip to Stockport to visit a former nanny. "I stayed there but Green drove my friend home. He was OK with us - friendly."

A Jean Worthington reported to the police. Again, she had nothing to report, only to say that she worked at the office at Carlton Ware and knew Leslie Green. "He would come to the office and wait for Mr Wiltshaw. On the day it happened, it was also my father's birthday and I went to see him that morning to say I hoped he had a good day. He was reading his newspaper. He looked up from his paper saying, 'Wait 'til you get to work!'."

Dr Harold Browne, who lived two doors away in Station Road added that everybody knew Mr and Mrs Wiltshaw. "They lived a quiet life and travelled a lot to Spain, which was why their house was called Estoril."

………………..

42

Going over what they had, Spooner was speaking to Millen.

"Everything indicates that robbery had been the murderer's motive. Everything also indicates that the murderer knew his way about the house and knew that Mrs Wiltshaw would be on her own there at that time."

"There was also a pair of blood-stained gloves found in the back garden – blood of Mrs Wiltshaw's group. The thumb of the left-hand glove had been newly torn." Miller replied.

"Almost certainly the murderer had dropped the glove as he ran away from the house. Where was he running to? Barlaston Station was only a seven minutes' walk away – three minutes if he ran!"

At this stage, theories were all we had to work on but one of our firmest hunches was that the murderer was no stranger to this fine house, called 'Estoril'.

Spooner continued, "This man, Leslie Green, had been chauffeur/gardener for the Wiltshaws, until he was sacked for using one of the Wiltshaw's cars without permission. He had used it on jaunts to go to Leeds, where he had a girl-friend.

Yes, Leeds…. that is significant. He would have had to come through Stafford to get to Barlaston from Leeds. Yes, Lockley had made the trip himself from Stafford to Barlaston and, according to him, Green would just about have had time to do the murder, - tight though - but that wasn't necessarily the case. We need proof."

…………………

Green appeared in Court on 27th July on the alleged charge of minor theft. The Court was crowded, but, as it happens, he owned up to the theft and the Hearing took only a minute. Superintendent W Crook asked for a remand in custody until next Wednesday stating that further inquiries had to be made and the remand was necessary.

…………..

For weeks we built up the case piece by piece like a jigsaw puzzle against Green. The Hearings for the petty thefts were basically repeatedly put off, with Green being remanded over and over, to give us time to get more information - but there was one gap we could not fill.

Amid the wealth of circumstantial evidence, some of it of the most damning kind – was how did Green get to Barlaston and get back without being seen?

We checked his movements on the day of the murder and rechecked. Except we couldn't account for the 55 vital minutes between the time Mrs Wiltshaw was last seen alive and when she was found dead by her husband in the hall of their beautifully furnished villa home.

Ideas that were paraded back and forth in the team were the possibility that he could have gone to Barlaston by bus, but he would have had a mile walk to and from the nearest bus stop, so that didn't fit. If he had travelled by train – and there were trains that would have suited his purpose both to and from Barlaston. Lockley had told us that the walk to Estoril would have taken seven minutes each way, less so if the murderer ran. Or did he use a stolen car or take a taxicab?

Employees and British Railways staff had not come up with anything concrete to help us at this time; every taxi driver in Stafford was questioned but no-one was found who took a passenger to Barlaston that afternoon. The police had no report of a car being stolen.

Another theory was that Green took a car from outside the Station Hotel, Stafford, drove to Barlaston and back and left the car where he had found it, without its being reported missing. "Somewhere there is a motorist who, on July 17th, was surprised to find that his car had used more petrol than he expected." one of the team put forward.

"But, if so, where was the car left in Barlaston?" Miller answered "Nobody has seen a strange car parked there."

Spooner was thinking pensively. "So, that leaves us back where we started with the murderer getting there by train. What's more, as those dropped gloves were found in the back garden, he could indeed have been heading for Barlaston Station – dropping them while running away from the back of the house."

So, working on the estimate of the pathologist's time of death Miller passed this information out to Barlaston station and found out that the murderer could have caught a local train to Stafford, connecting with the Holyhead express, which stopped at Leeds.

A PC presented Spooner with details about train times. It appeared there was a train from Stafford at 5.10, getting into Barlaston at 5.55, or one at 5.58 at Stafford, getting into Barlaston at 6.23. The train from Stafford to Leeds (a 73 mile journey) was one an hour at 5 minutes past the hour.

Reg Spooner pondered over the time-tables with Ernest Millen. Millen commented, "How long does it take to rob a terrified, defenceless woman, brutally murder her and make an escape?"

"We'll have to go over these charts carefully, Ernie. From what I can see, Stafford is 10 miles away from Barlaston. Look, Ernie… he could have caught the 5.10 train to Barlaston and returned on the 6.05, but it looks to me that he would only have had 15 minutes, if he'd run, before having to get back to Barlaston and catch the next train to Stafford, which seems almost impossible."

"So, it looks like we've got a case building here, what with the rubber-soles on his shoes and the cut on his left hand that exactly matches the glove found in the garden. What we need to do is find that RAF raincoat that was taken from the villa. I'll get our team to check all buses and trains out of Barlaston, although I know Lockley's team have done the same, but it's best to double-check to see whether it had been left on one. I'll get them to check with the Railway Police."

Miller went to Stafford to see the railway police. In particular, he was interested in that missing raincoat. He was sure it could have been of vital importance – enough to hang their suspect.

Detective Constable Harry Grimley, of the railway police at Stafford, was a formidable character, all 17 stone of him. "Right", he said, "I'll find your raincoat for you. I'll have the Permanent Way searched between Stafford and Holyhead. I'll have the left luggage office and lost property offices searched. I might as well have all the tickets checked to see if there is a ticket from Barlaston. Leave it to me, Ernie. I'll get in touch with you as soon as I find anything – now come and have a drink."

Miller accepted this invitation and also discovered that this formidable character also had a formidable capacity, and he came back from his session with Harry at the Stafford Station Hotel, full of confidence and hope, as well as beer.

A few days later, Harry Grimley came on the phone

"I've got it, the raincoat, but it wasn't on the Permanent Way."
"Are you sure it's the same raincoat." Miller asked.
"Of course it's yours – it's got three burns."

The raincoat, left on a rack of a compartment on the Stafford-Holyhead express, had been found at Holyhead on the same night as the murder and put in the lost property office.

"I've got it here", said Grimley, "and Ernie there are bloodstains on it."

The raincoat was later identified by Mr Wiltshaw and the blood was found to be that of his wife's group.

But Harry Grimley had got something more. He had found a ticket, bought at Barlaston, bought on 16th July and handed in at Leeds.

That seemed to confirm our theory that Leslie Green had gone to Leeds after the murder, probably to contact his girlfriend there.

Gradually we began to find out more about Green's movements.

During our interrogations, Green had told us that after he had been sacked by Mr Wiltshaw, he had a job as a chauffeur in Newcastle. He frequently visited his girlfriend in Leeds, a nurse called Nora Lammey, giving his name as Terry Green. He proposed to marry her.

He had made one of his visits to Leeds on July 8th, booking in at the Metropole Hotel as – incredibly – Mr L Wiltshaw of 'Estoril',

47

Barlaston. He stayed until July 12th but could not pay his hotel bill. He was given time to pay.

That night he left for London but on July 16th, the day of the murder, he was seen in Stafford, at lunchtime, and again at 6.35pm.

Nurse Lammey saw him again the next day, when he gave her two expensive rings, an eternity ring and a baguette ring. He had earlier paid off his £20 hotel bill.

But soon Nurse Lammey became uneasy, partly because of the sudden gift of rings and partly because of seeing later a newspaper report that police wanted to question a Leslie Green about the Wiltshaw murder. She showed him the newspaper but he denied it was anything to do with him. Nevertheless, she gave him back the rings.

It had taken about 1000 telephone calls and inquiries, including an interview with Nurse Lammey herself, to piece together Green's movements and track his comings and goings before and after the murder.

I, (Sergeant Millen) saw this as a classic case because of the way evidence was collected word by word from the murderer himself – especially from the lies he told on that first encounter of ours when he and I sat face to face for 10 long hours.

Some things Green did not know though. He did not know about that burned bloodstained mac and the ticket from Barlaston to Leeds. He did not know that the thumb of the left glove found in the garden at Estoril bore a cut, similar to the cut on Green's left thumb.

....

●Alf Robbins, left, in conversation with Detective Sergeant Ernest Millen, of New Scotland Yard, and his Stone colleague, Detective Constable Clarrie Morris.

Courtesy of Stoke Sentinel

Chapter 8

Visit to Constance Green

I, Supt Spooner and Detective Sergeant Millen paid a visit to Constance Green, Leslie Green's wife at 16 Elmore Avenue, Blurton. It was an old terraced house - two up, two down. Music was playing as she opened the door, it was 'Auf Wiederseh'n Sweetheart' by Vera Lynn.

Seeing us at the door, she just ran back into the house, saying, "I'll just turn the radio off." It looked like she was expecting us.

We let ourselves in. Constance was a petite blonde, probably dyed. We could hear a child playing out in the yard.

"I know what you're here about, it's my Leslie – well I say 'my' Leslie, even though he's hardly ever here and in fact, if you must have it, we have actually split up. He turned up, unexpected-like. .....Come to think of it, it must have been the day of the murder, in the early hours, about 2am. I was actually next door, but with all his shouting he woke me up.

He wasn't his normal self, quite demanding, like he'd grown a backbone! He quite blatantly asked for a divorce – said he had a girlfriend in Leeds and had proposed to her. Well, we had a terrific row and I called him all the names under the sun, asking how he thought we would be able to cope with no money coming in from him. All the years we'd been together and he was never so uncaring. I even threw a few things at him, then broke down crying but there wasn't a bit of sympathy from him. In the end I told him to get out and he went.

That's the last I saw of him until 22nd , yes it must have been Tuesday. I begrudgingly showed him the newspapers and told him you were looking for him. I told him he had to go see you, otherwise I'd tell the police myself.

Gillian, our daughter, came back from out playing with her friends. She was so pleased to see him, so he played with her. They were remembering Gillian's good friend, Jean Taylor, who she knew from Beeston Street, Sandford Hill, where Leslie had stayed for a while. Gillian would come over to visit and had met Jean there. Jean lived on a farm.

It was getting a bit late then so I offered him the settee for the night. The next morning he dressed, quite smartly for him, and obviously turned up at the police station, as I'd told him to.

 Anyway, sit down and I'll make you a cup of tea if you wish."

We looked at each other, "Yes, that would be most grateful, thank you."

When she was back I started by saying. "So, Mrs Green."
"Oh, call me Constance or Conny please. It's so formal being Mrs Green."

"Will do, ah'm … Constance. Now then, can you tell me about Leslie Green, in your own words. We want to get a general impression of him."

"Well, we met in 1945. He was in the army and I was in the WRENS. We met at a dance organised as we knew the war was finally coming to an end. He was a nice sort, polite and funny with it – had a great sense of humour – well he made me laugh and that's got a lot to do with how you get on together, if someone can make you laugh, don't you think? I knew he was a bit of a wild-un though, been in borstal a couple of times, so a bit of a lad, but I didn't mind that, although my mum was a bit wary. 'He's no good', she'd say. What's 'e gonna do when he gets out o' army?' I told her to give him a chance. Well, I'd fallen for him. So, we got married. Leslie had to go back to the army though – he still had a few years to serve – in the Highland Light Infantry he was. So I carried on living at my parent's place. Gillian was born in 1946. Anyway, we get this place in '48, and Leslie gets work as a driver. That's one thing borstal taught him, was how to drive.

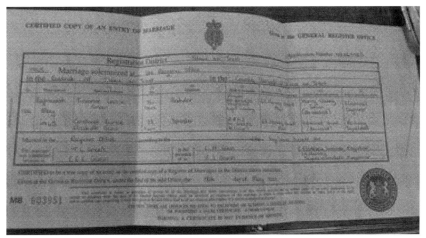

Wedding certificate for Terrance Leslie Green and Constance Eunice Elizabeth Gunn

Money was always tight as Leslie found it difficult sticking to a job. My mum was right, but I just thought he hadn't found his niche – you know, something that he liked, with people who liked him.

I think that Leslie was hoping that my father would get a job for him, but, they did not get on, mainly because Leslie is so unreliable – he could never get out of bed in time, for a start. So, Leslie has been doing all sorts of odd jobs, driving, night club attendant at the Cameo and such like. He'd sometimes be off for days at a time. He told me he had long-distance driving jobs. Come to think of it, it was always when he was short on cash and he'd get in a strange mood – not really himself, causing rows. Then he'd just disappear – never tell me he was going or when he was coming back. Then, when he gets back he tells me he was at the race tracks, trying to make a bit that way – more often losing everything on a nag instead. Still, if he couldn't win it, he'd rob it. That was him - always on the rob, ever since I knew him – to pay the mortgage. He'd bring back nice presents for me and Gillian, and food for a nice meal. So, I couldn't really have a go at him. He always provided for us in some way or the other.

We'd have a good time, going to the Duke of York, having a drink, playing darts – that's in Longton Road, Barlaston, or we'd go to the Feathers, you know The Plume of Feathers in Station Road, Barlaston meeting up with the lads and their ladies, tell a few jokes, have a laugh, as you do. My mum would look after Gillian.

Then he gets work as a chauffeur, come gardener, at the Wiltshaws. This was in 1950, and I thought he'd made it. It was a good job and I thought he would settle down at last.

But then he starts disappearing again at the weekends. He tells me he's been to Leeds for the racecourse at Wetherby but I had a feeling there was something else he wasn't telling me. I mean, why would he go to the races when he had a good job, earning good money? There had to be something else. Of course, I didn't know he had lost his job. It came as quite a shock. Then he disappears altogether. I don't see hide nor hair of him. I start thinking he's got someone else in tow – a floosy maybe. I was right, as he told me that day he wanted a divorce.

"Thank you for that, Constance," I answered. "Anyway, you know why we are here. We are investigating the murder of Mrs Wiltshaw, so we are questioning your husband as to his whereabouts on 16th July, the date of the murder. There was also quite a bit of expensive jewellery stolen."

"Well, as I said, he was here in the early hours, Tuesday night, 15th – I suppose that was actually then the 16th, that's all I can say, and he'd lost his job by then. I must say though that, although Leslie is a petty thief, and I wouldn't put it past him trying to rob the place, especially as he had been given the push, but as for murder.... Well, that's something completely different. Leslie wouldn't...... couldn't murder anyone in cold blood. That's just not him... it's not in his make-up. No.... you've got to find someone else for that. I mean, he's liked by everyone here – they wouldn't employ him – but everyone likes him – he's a laugh, one of the lads."

I thanked Constance for her candidness, and the tea, and we departed. We could hear strains of Here in My Heart by Al Martino, as Constance had turned the radio back on again.

Chapter 9

So, I was back in the holding cell, remanded over. So, just waiting. There was nothing to do but think. I could say I wasn't worried about the Wiltshaw murder. I hadn't done it. I hadn't even been near. But, I was worried - getting quite stressed in fact, even depressed, and my head ached. I hadn't had what you could call a good childhood, quite the opposite, with very bad memories that kept coming to the surface, especially when I was worried. I felt alone. With a growing feeling of helplessness. I started walking up and down my small cell. I had no-one to talk to, no-one to discuss my worries with. They wanted to pin a murder on me – something I didn't do.

In my worried state, the childhood memories came flooding back. Dad was strict, no talking at the dinner table (if there was anything much to eat that is) no laughing, sit up straight, don't put too much food in your mouth at one time, close your mouth when you are eating, no elbows on the table. If he saw fit to reprimand me, he would. One day I knocked a glass of water over when reaching for the salt. Ma went to right the glass and was going to get a cloth, "Hold yew hard, ma." Dad stared at me over the table – a cold,empty stare. I wanted to get up and run, but daren't. "Reet Terrance," dad finally voiced. "Ent it tarm yer larnt to du summat wi'out upskelling owt. Tarm I learnt ye a lesson, me lad." And he was going for his belt again. Mum tried to intervene but all she got was "Stop mitherin' me. 'Ee needs te larn – 'e's nay bairn."

I started to cry, before the slap of the leather hit me, holding my hands up to try to hold him back, but he'd grabbed me by the hair and ....well, I don't remember anymore. I remember the pain the next morning, as I lay in my bed. I don't remember getting to bed. There were many times like that, when I just didn't remember getting hit by my dad. I began to think this was normal and that everybody lost time. I'd often heard my mother say, "I don't know wheer tarm 'as gone," or "Tarm seems te 'ave sped by an' I've so much te do?"

A little later, dad just up'd and disappeared. He never came back. Mum thought he had gone to London. At first I thought it was my fault - that he'd had enough of me doing things wrong, but mum assured me that she was pleased he had gone, but that it would be even more difficult now with no money coming in from him. I was pleased he'd scarpered too as he was just a big bully. To me he was dead, gone from my world. I'd even written on my marriage certificate that he was deceased.

Mum had to take in washing and sewing work to try to make ends meet. She'd be up all day and most of the night, straining her eyes over this needlework, trying to get it done in time, otherwise she wouldn't get paid enough. Mum called it piece work and had to explain that she had to make so many pieces of finished work in a set time. Trouble is there was never enough time. There was also never enough food on the table and I could see mum getting thinner and weaker as the weeks went on. I was a thin runt myself.

This was no way to live, so I started going around the shops and nicking stuff while the shop-keeper wasn't looking. I'd pay for something mum had given me money to buy, then pocket other stuff while the shop-keeper had his back to me at the till. I didn't run away, as that would have meant he'd be running after me, possibly catch me and I'd be for the high jump. No, I just stood there, waiting for my change, and nonchalantly saunter off. I got quite handy at doing that, plus pocketing the odd purse I'd see in an open handbag or a wallet popping out of a back trouser pocket.

I couldn't keep in the same area though as people had become wary, so went a bit further afield sometimes. I went to school sometimes, sometimes I didn't.

It was great to get home, after school, and see mum's smile as she looked at the goodies I had brought home. She called me her cherub.

My uncle then started coming over – mum's brother. He would help out where he could – but I didn't like him. He was an evil so-and-so, like my father, calling me Terrance all the time.

He'd stay over some nights, drinking the evening away, like my dad. That's when I found out what a sod he could be and he'd come to my room, reeking of beer, put his hands under the covers and start playing with my bits. I tried often enough the cry out for my mum, but he'd put a hand over my mouth, then lie on top of me. I tried to bite him, but he was too strong and heavy. "Now, Terrance, be good en stop wriggling, en ye dare tell yer ma and yer'll get woss – I'll kill yer, en I mean it."

I have memories or another time when he actually twirled me over onto my front, hoist me up onto my knees and penetrated me from the back. I was crying and trying to scream, but the screams just wouldn't come out through my sobbing.

I tried to tell mum, but mum wouldn't listen. "Yer've nivver liked yer uncle, and now yer meking up stories about 'im. Yer turning inte a right little tyke. I've nivver 'eard of the likes. 'E's bin kind to us, your uncle, yer should be grateful.

Things got worse as now mum wasn't on my side. She wouldn't talk to me anymore, just shove a plate of food in front of me and say, "Theer, that's what yer uncle got ye. All yer snivelling,ugh!

I don't remember any more, just that some mornings I'd wake up and I was sore down there. If he did do it again, I must have blanked it out, gone into my own little world. I don't remember much at all. I had no good memories, feeling very low, miserable and helpless. I had no interest in anything and just felt that life was worthless – that I was worthless, taking it on board what my dad had said, that I was a good for nothing. I didn't do well at school and had no friends. All my classmates seemed to avoid me.

Then my uncle stopped coming around.

I thought I would be alright now. I started stealing again, until one day I came home and there was a strange man there. I suppose I must have been about 11. Mum introduced him as George and said that George would be helping to pay the bills so she wouldn't have to work so hard and I didn't have to go stealing anymore. She didn't want me getting caught, although I had a feeling she was never going to be that loving mother ever again and wouldn't bother if I was sent away.

"Whatever," I thought to myself, rather despondently and went to play with my wooden toy train.

Mum and George went upstairs. I heard mum say I'd be alright playing downstairs. I wondered what they were going upstairs for but didn't think much more about it. I know I was playing quite loudly, bashing the furniture with the train and making 'woo woo' noises, like a train engine. Then, all of a sudden, this gruff voice shouted down the stairs for me to "pack it in with that sodding row, sithee." I stopped in my tracks, quite literally, and started to cry. No-one had shouted at me since dad had gone. "Stop that wailing, you brat," came the harsh voice again and George came rushing down the stairs, picked me up by the collar and shoved me in the cupboard under the stairs.

…. Then I hear the clomp, clomp, clomp back up the stairs and a door slam. It was pitch black and I could see nothing through my tears. Dead quietness. I started shouting, "Let me out, let me out" screaming, screaming, screaming and banging on the door. No-one came. I was so scared and started thinking. What if he had killed my mum? What if I never get out of here? Am I going to die? I was sweating profusely. I'd always been frightened of the dark from ever since I could remember and mum used to leave the passage light on. I felt as if the cupboard was starting to spin around, even though I couldn't see anything, just a glimpse of light at the top of the door, swirling round and around. I couldn't breathe. I think I must have passed out.

The next thing I remember I was at school. The teacher was bringing around the results of a maths test we had done. I had no memory of doing this maths test and no memory of getting to school that day, or getting out of the cupboard. I looked at the top of the paper, at the date, and it was a whole week later! "You've done well in the test, Leslie" the teacher addressed me. "So much better than you've ever done before, especially as you're hardly ever here. Anyway, well done, plus you've been here every day this week. I think you deserve a gold star." I remember thinking, 'I hate maths, how comes I've done well - and I've no memory of the past week at all?' The teacher returned, "I just wanted to add that I noticed you had put Terrance Leslie Green on the top of the paper. You're down in our records as just Leslie Green. I will have to speak to your mother to see if our records need changing."

"Oh, don't do that, Miss." I pleaded, "I must have just been day-dreaming. I'm called Terrance or Terry sometimes, but...(I was going to say that it was only when I had been naughty, but stopped in mid-sentence), but only as a lark. Sorry Miss."

I still never understood that incident. George kept coming round but I didn't play up again. I was so scared of him and was as quiet as a mouse when he was there. He'd left me with a great dread of dark, cramped places. There was food on the table and mum looked a bit happier, although there seemed to be a sadness in her eyes and I noticed some bruising on her arms. "Oh, nowt to werrit yersen about, now then me lad. I keep bashing mesel ont doors, that's all. It's me eyesight from all that sewing I did."

George stopped coming around when mum started getting bigger round the belly.

I remember the School Board came round one day about me missing so much school. They inspected the place and questioned my mum. Finding out that my dad had flown the nest, and that mum was struggling, they referred me to the Leeds authorities, who sent me off to Shadwell Approved School after the magistrates had decided that I was "a juvenile in need of care and protection. It was alright there. I felt fairly safe. There was a stability to the place with their rules and regulations and I even made some friends. I don't know how long I was there but they let me out some time later. Mum must have got a job or getting on a bit better. Anyway, when I came home from Shadwell, it was to find out that I had a baby sister. I didn't much like her. She cried all the time and couldn't talk – couldn't do much really, just eat, poop and cry.

Chapter 10

That memory had left me even more anxious. I had to get it out of my head but there was nothing to do in the holding cell apart from think. I got up, did some exercises, then slumped back on the bed. There was a lot of shouting going on – just other prisoners acting up.

I began day-dreaming again.

There was a bit more money around than before the war. Soldiers had money and were in the mood to spend it, notoriously at the race courses, where Charlie, Lorenzo and I would go too, but not to spend. We were preying on bookmakers (with their bulging satchels), and punters alike, at railway stations and racecourse car parks. We'd all learnt our trade, as kids, as pickpockets, so that's what we did. There were loads around, including the card sharps and three-card tricksters, who plied their trade. However, gone were the race gangs who terrorised the street, the racecourses, as well as each other!

Yes, the police had come down heavy on them after a violent gunfight between the London Sabini gang and the Brummagem Boys from Birmingham. I wasn't even born yet at the time but I heard about it later on.

I heard that, on June 2, 1921, after the Epsom races that day, the Birmingham Boys ambushed a charabanc containing bookmakers from Leeds, ramming it with a taxi.

The gang attacked the passengers with hammers, hatchets, bottles and bricks, hospitalising six with head wounds. Of the 28 gang members arrested, 23 were jailed, and Billy Kimber's reign as king of the underworld was over.

It used to be that on many racecourses, particularly in the cheaper rings and in open areas distant from the grandstands, pitches were allocated not by right, but might. I saw them, before the war. Bookmakers often had no choice but to share their profits with these gangsters, and to pay for the services they offered - protection, lists of runners, chalk, sponges and buckets of water, wanted or not. Sometimes the gang would charge bookmakers as much as 50 per cent of their profits for the privilege of conducting their business unmolested. Sometimes, bookmakers were asked to contribute to a charity – of course the charity was the gang themselves – and if they didn't – well they'd receive a good going-over. It was no good reporting these gangs to the police as the gang-members would just cover up for each other, giving alibis and so forth.

I admit there was a gang I got in with in Leeds. They were not like the big gangs down south, just really street gangs, fighting amongst themselves mainly for territory rights – that meant that no member of a gang dare to go into the territory of another gang on his own, otherwise he might not come out alive. I learnt my pickpocketing skills from them. If you lived on those streets, you were OK and protected by that particular gang, but any strangers coming into the area were followed, with knives and razors flashing, cat-called and basically made so scared that they were glad to get out of the area.

These gangs would wait outside factory gates on payday to fleece the workers of their hard-earned cash, making an average of £75 to £100 a day.

The older ones were able to remember William Plommer, who on 27th April 1925 waded into a fistfight and was fatally stabbed outside his home. In July that year, the brothers Wilfred and Lawrence Fowler were convicted of Plommer's murder and sentenced to death at West Riding Assizes in Leeds. They were hanged two months later.

I would go around with one of these gangs. Things were getting worse for the gangs as unemployment had risen and their profits had fallen. On one night a big fight broke out between them, with each side throwing bricks, waiting for the other gang to come in closer to feel the blades of their razors and knives. Some had cudgels, which they'd hardened with tar. It was a sort of tit-for-tat, trying to get money off the other gang.

I was there with a few pals about my age and we were doing our bit to harass the other gang. I'd got myself a big stick and was throwing stones, defending ourselves with dustbin lids. It was an all-out fight. I was only small for my age but, even though I was scared, a voice inside me seemed to be urging me on to fight and maim and really hurt the blighters. I could feel this other me making me stronger and angrier, so enraged – this voice was shouting, "kill 'em, kill 'em!" I got down amongst the multitude of kicking feet, trying to trip up the opposition and bring them down, so I could pounce on them and bring my cosh down on their heads. I succeeded in bringing one man down and was just about to swipe his cloth-capped head with a hefty blow, and see the blood ooze over the pavement, when suddenly, I felt a big sooty coal sack being thrown over my head and arms. I couldn't move, I couldn't breathe – dark and enclosed –the cupboard under the stairs encroached into my thoughts. I was struggling to be let out and screaming. Then I was kicked, over and over. I was in such pain, and crying. I think I must have passed out.

I don't remember much else as the next thing I remember was being back at school again. The thing is, I was in a different class and a different teacher. I was in clean clothes. I looked to see if I had bruises, but any I had must have healed. I was trying to follow what the teacher was saying, but I was lost, nothing made sense to me. I looked around and sort of recognised school friends, but they seemed to be a bit bigger and taller than before. Nothing seemed to fit. To my astonishment, I found out later that I had lost a year. I had lost a year from my memory. I was in the next year up. There was no way of catching up for a lost year. The teacher was asking me questions about things I should have known, but I didn't. He was very disappointed so, at the end of that school year, I was made to remain in the same class. All of my friends went up a year, so I lost contact with them. I was again very alone, very lost.

Mum had started on the sewing again and taking in washing, and I started thieving again. I got away with it for quite a few years, up until when I got caught.

I was clumsy. It was cold and my fingers had gone numb, but I saw this shiny, leather wallet sticking out of a back pocket and made a lunge for it. It slipped out of my hands and the fellow whipped round and grabbed me.

That's when I ended up in Thorp Arch Approved School, leaving when I was 16, in 1939.

Borstal wasn't all that bad, although it was hard work. We were expected to do a solid eight hours' work each day but could receive training in a wide variety of practical skills such as carpentry, sheet-metal work, bricklaying, boot- and shoe-making, farming, horticulture and cookery. That's where I learnt to drive and do engine repairs.

The inmates were allocated to houses, with up to 50 in each group, so I made some good friends. We had to pass through a series of three grades. The first grade, which lasted about six months included a period of preliminary training and observation. In the second grade you obtained privileges, so that you could join certain clubs, or the Cadet Force, or to go on occasional escorted walks or outings. Once you'd earnt trust, you were then promoted to the third grade, where you had status. They allowed you to work without supervision, go on walks on your own or to the local cinema or youth club, take charge of a party of junior boys and, finally, become eligible for home leave.

For miscreants, corporal punishment was explicitly excluded, instead the options included reduction in privileges, reduction in grade, restriction in diet, stoppage of earnings, or a period of confinement to a cell.

A strict routine of early starts, hard labour and exercise. The day started at 6am with a run – often in the pouring rain – then press-ups and sit-ups followed by a breakfast of bread and jam or porridge. The inmates were then set to work such as scrubbing and cleaning the floors, as well as laundry and cooking meals.

Lunch was followed by work including carpentry, forestry, baking and gardening, before lessons with the prison's educational officer.

After tea they had an hour of rugby training followed by 'quiet time and diaries' before being given supper and bed.

The strict rules meant it was forbidden for inmates to swear, disrespect officers, be lazy or careless, disobey orders or make unnecessary noise.

Of course I tried to obey the rules. There was no way I was going to get punished and be confined to a cell. Those nightmares still haunted me, but I didn't want to be thought of as a cissy either. A couple of the lads had started taunting me - started calling me names, because I was small, quiet and kept to myself. Then someone punched me on the shoulder and I turned round and whacked him – an uppercut, right under the chin, that sent him sprawling.

Next minute I was being grabbed by the charge-hands and dragged into a small, dark, room. "There, young man, you can cool off inside there. There's no fighting allowed."

"But, I dint start it."

"You're the one who threw a punch, so take your just deserts."

I don't really remember much of what happened after that. Everything went black. I know no-one must have picked on me again, as I didn't get thrown into that tiny, dark room again. I suppose I must have finished the course at Thorp Arch Approved School but it all seems to be a bit of a blur now, as if walking around in a dream. There were times when I remember doing field work, times when I was allowed to go to the cinema on my own, times when I was let out, back home for a visit, but I had no memory of getting back from the field work or getting to the cinema or even how I got home. I know people started saying I'd done things that I had no recollection of doing. People started calling me Terrance. I asked them why, "Oh, don't you remember, you nincompoop." someone called Jim answered, "You got quite narky and mithered the other day – you had a right lem on (angry) and said, 'I'm not Leslie, I'm Terrance', so, we started calling you Terrance."

"What was I narky about?"

"Oh, Piggy here was trying to nick some food off your plate, and you turned right nasty-like. We thought you were going to cop 'im one, but you saw the guards looking, and sat down again. You had a right cob on you. Yer face turned kind of frightening to look at, like the Hulk in the comics, but not green – sure scared Piggy."

"Oh, was all I could say." I knew something was wrong. I wasn't stupid, I'd passed all of my training courses. I'd found myself, many a time, floating in and out of blackness. But, I didn't want to see a doctor – I was frightened they'd send me off to some asylum or other – tell me I was mentally incapable, insane even – even give me a lobotomy. No, I'd just have to put up with it and try to hide my blackout spells, cover them up with lies – make up stories of what I'd been doing. I'd become quite ingenious in improvisation, feigning knowledge of what I did not know. Somehow, it seemed the older I got, the worse things became.

War had been announced when I got out. It was 1939. Thorp Arch had recommended I join the army. I was 16, so old enough to enlist, so I decided to join the Highland Light Infantry.

There was a lot of initial training, marching; fitness training, which involved clambering over walls and nets and through tunnels; a lot of cross-country running carrying heavy rucksacks; learning how to shoot with a rifle, and being able to take a rifle apart and put it together, blindfolded.

Of course, I wasn't the blue-eyed boy in the army. There's something in me that always makes me stray. I was imprisoned for theft in 1940, in Glasgow. I got 60 days. Then I got sent to Dunkirk in northern France as part of Operation Dynamo.

It was my first operation on foreign soil. We were all scared silly, being bombed on the beach, by the Bosch. Because of the shallow waters, our destroyers were unable to approach the beaches.

We had nowhere to hide and my friends, colleagues and hundreds of thousands of different battalions that had been landed on the beach, were dying in their droves around me. The noise of the bombs whistling overhead, the boom, boom of the guns with bullets splintering around me, within arms-reach, one whizzed right by me and I felt blood running down my cheek – luckily it was only a flesh wound. I had managed to wade out onto the beach and threw myself face-down, burying my head in the sand, pulling the sand over me and try to hide, waiting for my turn to feel that searing pain of a bullet or bomb wrack my body, leaving me dead or wounded. I hadn't even fired a single shot.

I had flashing images of when I was a kid, locked in that cupboard under the stairs, sweating, not able to breathe, everything spinning. I have no memory after that. I must have passed out, semi-suffocated in the sand. Maybe someone dragged me away but the next I knew, I was on a ship, going back to England. I knew my face was bleeding but I knew I was really grateful to whoever had dragged me off that beach – they'd saved my life. I relaxed and slept the rest of the journey to Ramsgate, then I and the remnants of my regiment and other soldiers were transported to Southend.

We stayed in Southend for quite a while, recovering, getting new kit, then acting as a holding company. There was a lovely lady who made us cheese and bread with lots of cups of tea. She couldn't cope with even more of us descending on her and had run out of crockery. So, me being me, I stole a huge lump of cheese and some butter for her, as a way of saying thank you. Each morning the bagpipes sounded and we paraded up and down the road.

Anyone reading the Courier and Advertiser on Friday, 30th May 1941, will have found out that I had got myself into trouble again.

'Deserter, posed as Corporal, jailed.'

I'd had enough of the army and wanted out. There was talk of us being sent abroad again and I'd had my fill of war. I got listed as a deserter. What happened was, we were stationed in Dundee. A platoon of Canadian forces were stationed with us. I'd got drunk and got into a wicked sort of mood. Only play-acting, but I wanted a laugh. So, I snuck into the Canadian billet at night and nicked the uniform of a corporal in the Canadian forces. Then I ran off into the night.

I did have a giggle to myself, dressing up in the corporal's uniform, admiring the stripes. I felt great – not just a lowly private anymore – I was something. In fact, a couple of Canadian privates saw me, and actually saluted. That was a good feeling. Of course, it didn't last, but I got that first perception of not being me, but someone better, someone to be respected and looked up to. It was a strange feeling, dream-like, as if I were looking down on myself from another body. Another body that was acting on my behalf, but I wasn't actually doing or saying what this other person was saying or doing. The other person was strutting around like a peacock, looking cock-a-hoop and enjoying the notoriety of the theft and the pride in being what I can only say as, being respected, as a corporal. I put it all down to the booze. I was woozy.

The MPs were after me. This other person, in my body, stole a revolver and pointed it at the officers. There was no chance though and one of them managed to hit me over the head with a rifle butt and I found myself in a glasshouse in Northumberland. When I got out I had no memory of what I had done and wondered why people kept calling me Terry, not Terrance, like in Borstal, but Terry. Others had to tell me what I had been accused of and someone shouted out that I had said my name was Terry. I figured it must have been the blow to my head. Of course, I got charged with desertion but the charge also included that:

(1) between May 17 and 19, 1941, in the hostel, 5 Golden Square, Aberdeen, I had stolen a revolver;

(2) on May 19, at the servicemen's hostel, Dudhope Street, Dundee, I was found in possession of two revolvers and 20 rounds of ammunition without holding a firearms certificate; and

(3) I had worn shoulder-emblems with the word, "Canada", corporal's stripes, buttons and caps worn by members of the Canadian forces, while not authorised to do so.

I was going to be kicked out of the army. I was sentenced to one month's imprisonment by Sheriff Macdonald at Dundee yesterday. I was hoping they'd throw me out of the army, but in the middle of a world war, that wasn't going to happen. I was finally released from the glasshouse and sent back to my unit.

Chapter 11

Of course, I'd grown up a bit since those days and I wasn't like that anymore. Yes, I was still a thief, but I didn't harm anyone, just out for a bit of fun. I was that likeable, funny guy – a bit of a rogue, but genial. I had my wife and daughter, although I think it was too late to try to save the marriage, especially as I was bound to go to jail again for petty theft and I didn't think she'd forgive me about Nora. That was one step too far.

I'd had enough just sitting here, going over my past life. It was just making me depressed. I was frightened that the police would try to pin this murder on me, not having found anyone else to fit the bill – me a low time crook. I knew they were trying to build a case against me, keeping me so long on a larceny charge. I mean what good was I to society, split from his wife, no fixed abode, not able to keep a job. A low down bum. Easy to blame this murder on me. Easy to get rid of me!

I was due at the Magistrates' Court on Wednesday, 31st July on the charge of larceny. The courtroom was packed but I was only there a minute as Supt W Crook asked for a further remand in custody until next Wednesday. He stated that further inquiries had to be made and the remand was necessary. I was asked if I wanted to apply for legal aid and, I don't know why but I again refused.

I asked to speak to Supt Lockley, who duly came to Stone to see me.

"I dint do the murder, Supt Lockley, although I know I am involved and perhaps responsible in an indirect way. I just want to give you my side of it."

"OK, go on,"

"Well, I now remember what I did on Tuesday, July 15th. (*I'd had time to think up a story of what I'd been doing in London – it wasn't much, but it would fit the bill. Some of it I did remember doing but other bits were vague.*)

So, I went from the Strand Palace Hotel, in London, int' morning, with me bag, to Euston Railway Station, and put me bag int' left luggage. This must have been near midday. I went back to busy part of town, where all the theatres are, and just walked rarnd. I went back to Euston between 3pm and 3.30pm and walked rarnd station 'aving a gander at the shops, stalls and diesel engines on show while the train was due in, at 5pm.

I booked through to Crewe and I got theer wi'out changing trains, just after 8pm. I booked in at the Railway Station Hotel theer and then walked up to town centre and went to t'theatre. Theer is only one theatre in t'town. I forget the name of the show but I remember there was a conjurer with a beer barrel act and a comedian and some dancing girls who came on first.

I came out half way through. It wasn't really my cuppa tea. I went back to me hotel to get some food, but I codna get any and was directed to a café for some scran. I had some bacon, egg and chips and got back to my hotel at 11pm. I mooched around int lounge for a while, looking at some magazines, then went to bed."

"So, why did you break your journey, why did you get out at Crewe?"

"Well, I was ont way yam to Longton (*that was an expression used in Stoke too, meaning 'home' so Lockley understood me*) and, as I had to change at Crewe, I decided to stay. I cod've got yam, I suppose, but I codna make up my mind what to do. To explain why I was in such a state – well, I'd been seeing Nora Lammey, she's a nurse in Leeds and we were getting quite serious. I 'ad proposed to 'er, but I was still married, so I 'ad to see my lass, Constance, to tell her all of this, and to ask for a divorce. I knew this werrent going to be easy and I s'pose I was scared of consequences. Constance were going to be vexed and even shrike (cry)..... I'd even asked my pals Lorenzo and Charlie to look for two rings for me. I was going to give 'em to Nora.

The next morning I 'ad some coffee and went to the railway station. I waited quite a bit for a train but it finally arrived at abart 11am and eventually got to Stafford at 11.45.

I left me bag at t'station and walked rarnd until I went to the Station Hotel at half-past one.

"Why did you go to Stafford?"

"Oh, like I said, I just codna make up my mind what to do. I was in a bit of a state, flummoxed you might say. The more I thought abart it, I dint know what to do. I dint know whether to go yam (home) or go to Newcastle and eventually I decided to go back to Leeds. I've already told you all about that. I went to t'Station Hotel and had dinner."

"So, you chickened out of speaking to your wife?

"Yes."

"Just to confirm," Lockley interrupted, "So, this was 16th July and you were in Stafford, having dinner at the Station Hotel?"

"Yes, sir. I suppose I finished dinner about 3.30pm. I'd 'ad a few drinks after the meal. I was making my way to the station and came over really tired. I'm not a great one for drinking in t'afternoon – it goes to me 'ead, see. I sat missen darn (*sat myself down*) on a park bench, and must have fallen asleep. I don't remember anything else until I woke up just before 6.30. I decided to go back to t'hotel. (*This is what I remember, falling asleep on a park bench.*)

Just before you ask, nooo I didna meet anyone in Stafford I knew and I dote know anybody theer."

"You mentioned meeting a "Lorenzo" and "Charlie". Where do you know these people from?"

"I've known Lorenzo, I s'pose, for about two month or maybe a bit more. I'd got me a job in a nightclub for a while – the Cameo in Longton. I met Lorenzo there three or four times, and 'ave seen him elsewhere in Leeds three or four times. Lorenzo had come up to me in the Cameo one night –'e'd recognised me as we'd shared the same cell in a prison some years ago. 'E's a wrong-un too – petty thief that is. 'E'd suggested a couple of break-in and entering jobs. We once went to Huddersfield together in Lorenzo's car, to do a warehouse job, but it dint come off."

"Do you know where this Lorenzo can be found?"

"Sorry, I dote know where he lives and I dote know what bars he visits in Leeds, but I did see 'im int bar of the Hotel Metropole. If he wanted to get in touch with me he knew I'd either be at the Cameo, in Longton, or the Metropole in Leeds, because he knew I stayed there quite often. I've no way of contacting him or where to find him. Lorenzo – well, that's his surname, I believe, but it's the only name I have known him by. He's abart 42 or 43 years old. I would say he's 5ft 8in tall, well built, 'as dark hair, straight and very thick, parted on one side. E's clean-shaven, 'as a pale complexion and a round face. Most of times I've seen 'im e's been wearing dark clothes – no 'at. I actually think e's a southerner. 'E likes 'is jewellery and 'as a gold wrist watch on a gold chain strap."

74

"What about Charlie."

"Charlie is abart 32 years old, abart six feet, pale, wi' a thinnish face, thinnish build, clean-shaven, allus reasonably well dressed and likes to wear a turned-darn trilby.

"So, did Lorenzo and Charlie get you the two rings you required?"

"Yes, sir. Lorenzo also gave me a few bits of gold and a gold cigarette case. I sold the cigarette case and a gold chain int' jeweller's shop in Vicar Lane."

"So, had you discussed with Lorenzo and Charlie, the possibility of a robbery at Estoril?"

"As like as mebbee. They knew I 'ad worked there and I'd mentioned there was jewellery int 'ouse. They may 'ave got the rings from theer, but I'm not saying they did. I wasn't with 'em. Maybe they 'ad another man with 'em."

"Ok, Green. As you know, Supt Spooner is leading this investigation and will be interviewing you further."

. . . .

My memory of meeting Lorenzo and Charlie in Leeds was playing out in my mind, as a scenario, as I spoke to Supt. Lockley.

I remember meeting them at the Metropole Hotel in Leeds. We had lunch together. Lorenzo wanted to do a job.

"Hey, Leslie, I hear where you work in Barlaston, the people are loaded. I'm getting a bit short of reddies."

75

"Well, the missus allus wears loads of jewellery, that's a fact."

"I think they're due a little visit, what do yer think? Are you up for it?"

I dunno, Lorenzo. I've got a good little job theer and I dote want to lose it. It's the first long-time job I've 'ad. I dote want to muck it up. – sorry, count me out."
"Aw, you gone soft on us, Leslie?"

"Me soft – nooo, but as I said, not this time, not wheer I work, that's too close for comfort, yer dote shit on yer own doorstep – another job mebbee."

"Well, maybe you can give us the low-down on how to get there, best time to go, and where to find the jewels."

No, I don't want to be involved, Lorenzo."

"Ok, let me know if you change your mind."

A bit later, I got sacked by the Wiltshaws for borrowing the car too many times, so I was up Shit Street wi'out a paddle, as the saying goes.

The next time Lorenzo and Charlie popped into the Metropole I told them I needed money as I'd been sacked.

"Well, you've no problem doing the job with us then – there'll be no comeback." Lorenzo replied.

"Nooo, as like as mebbee I'd be called in for questioning. With my background they'll lock me up and lose the key, just for having worked for the Wiltshaws. No, I still dote want to be involved. It *will be a great haul for you two – I just want a few things and some money for messen."*

So I told Lorenzo and Charles what they needed to know, saying a couple of nice rings would come in handy too, for my girlfriend. They were to let me know when they were going to do the job and I'd make sure I was well away from the place.

Lorenzo and Charlie discussed their plan for a bit, then came back with, "How's about 16th July? Going on what you said, we'll be there at around 5.30 in the afternoon. We'll meet up with you here on 17th July."

"Fine, I'll make sure I'm nowheer near the place on 16th."
"Ok, we'll all meet at the Stafford Hotel on 16th to make final arrangements and you can go your own way from there."

"I'll probably go back to Leeds and I'll see you there."

So, on 17th July Lorenzo, Charlie and I met up in Leeds.
"'Ere, Leslie, we managed to get you a few things." He was straight-faced, not smiling and hovering a bit distance from me, which I felt strange for him. "Here, we got you two lovely rings, which were grabbed off the old lady's fingers, a gold cigarette case and a gold chain. There's a few quid for you too."

"Owd it go?"

I remember Lorenzo looking quizzically at me, then finally replied, haltingly, ".....You don't need to know."

I pondered a bit on that. Normally Lorenzo would be looking cook-a-hoop, but he wasn't, and neither was Charlie.

Still, I had a bit of money in my pocket now and a couple of lovely rings for Nora.

…………..

Lorenzo and Charlie walked off. "You do gather from that, Charlie, that Leslie has no idea he was there and did the nasty?"

"Yer, he's a right 'eadcase (said while twirling his middle finger at the side of his head). The same as when he broke the arm of the guy at the Cameo then threw him down the stairs."

"That's right. Exactly the same. I think we'd better make ourselves scarce, Charlie me lad, cos the shits gonna 'it the fan. We'll go down south or even abroad. We've got money and jewels we can hock."

Chapter 12

So, it was Supt Spooner's turn. Supt Lockley spoke to him beforehand. "Green's just given me a cock and bull story of what he had been doing before and at the time of the murder."

"Well, he's had plenty of time to make something up, hasn't he?" replied Supt Spooner.

"Hmm, but the only story he managed to come up with to account for his whereabouts around the time of the murder was that he fell asleep on a park bench in Stafford, after a boozy lunch. Surely he could have thought up something better than that, I ask you!"

"Never, is he the full quid or what? A six-year old boy could have come up with something more believable!"

"He says he was involved though, but didn't do the murder. He said he got two rings from friends called Lorenzo and Charlie, implying these two, with a possible third man, did the robbery and murder."

"The third man being himself, no doubt." Spooner countered.

"There was something else I picked up on though. He said he 'chickened out' from seeing his wife, and we know he saw her as you've spoken with Constance Green.

"So, he's got a bad memory as well, not good for a small-time crook."

"He's a strange man, Reg. Tell me what you think after this interview. He's got a good line in half-truths, mixed with a good pinch of make-believe, I can tell you that, apart from his tall tale of about the park bench! It seems very strange to me, though, coming up with the most convoluted of stories then, all of a sudden, he's asleep on a park bench!"

"Yes, we've got to find out if Lorenzo and Charlie actually exist or are a figment of his imagination."

"You'd think he would want to protect them if they actually exist, but he gave such vivid descriptions of them, as though he wants us to find them."

"Perhaps he's scared he's in too deep and wants to dob them in to get off the murder charge."

"Perhaps."
……………..

So, Supt Spooner and I (Sergeant Millen) interviewed Green again, on 23rd July. He gave us a bit more background in a much longer statement. He described having seen an advertisement in the Sentinel for a chauffeur/handyman at the Wiltshaws' house. He was paid £7 a week and had a uniform provided. He worked for Mr Wiltshaw until May 1952 when he was given a week's notice for using the car without permission. He used to go to work in old army clothes and change in the garage.

After he left Estoril, he got a job as a bricklayer's labourer. He and his wife were buying their own house through a building society and to help with the money his wife worked as well. He then started to work as a van driver for Garners, seedsmen at Newcastle. He stayed with them until three weeks ago, when he left.

Sometime in May 1952 he met a girl called Nora Lammey at the Astoria Dance Hall in Leeds. She was the same age as him and told him that she was a nurse. He introduced himself as 'Terry' and from then on he met the girl regularly, telling her that he was single. When he left Garners, he returned home to his family and travelled back to Leeds at weekends. He then flew to Belfast where Nora Lammey's parents lived and spent two or three days with her there. When he flew back, he booked in at the Metropole Hotel, Leeds, under the name of L Wiltshaw of Estoril, Barlaston.

On Saturday,12th he saw Nora in the afternoon and at 2.40am the following morning he caught the train to London, where he booked into the Stand Hotel under the name of Colin Jones.

The journey to London appears to have been somewhat pointless for he was soon back on the train, this time to Stafford, on 16th July, from where he said that he hoped to go home to patch things up with his wife. At the Station Hotel, Stafford, he chatted to one or two people and at 3.30pm went into the dining room. He stayed in the hotel drinking and then left at about 5pm, going into a nearby park where he sat down and dozed off. He then went back to the Metropole Hotel in Leeds."

I discussed this statement with Supt Spooner afterwards, asking "Where did he get the money for all this travelling?"

"Who know, petty theft and the like, I suppose. He could even have done some breaking and entering with this Lorenzo and Charles – if they exist that is."

We continued re-reading the statement. Green was saying that he stayed at the Metropole Hotel until Sunday evening (20th), spending most of his time with Nora Lammey. Telling Nora that he had to go to Torquay on business, he left his girlfriend at 3am on the Monday (21st) and made two more aimless journeys, first to Newton Abbot and then to Shrewsbury, from where he telephoned Nora and arranged to meet her in Birmingham, as she was travelling down on her way to Stourbridge. They parted at

7.30pm, after which he caught a train to Stafford and arrived at his home at about 2am. Unable to wake anyone in the house, he spent the night in the outside toilet until 8am, when his wife, who had been staying next door, came home. The final words of the statement were, "I was not in Barlaston or in fact near Barlaston or Stafford on Wednesday afternoon, July 16th.

This statement took over four hours to complete.

On 24th July, Green, having had the night to think things over, gave a third, more detailed statement to the police:

"I am clear in my mind what I did on Wednesday 16th July 1952. I know I arrived at Stafford railway station round about 10am on the Wednesday morning and round about 1.30pm went to the Station Hotel. I went into the hotel bar and noticed two men talking to the barman [actually the hotel manager]. Two other men came up and I remained with the four of them until 3.30pm, then we ordered lunch and went into the dining room.

We finished around 4.30pm and then went into the upstairs lounge. We stayed for quarter of an hour and then I began to feel dizzy from the drink I had taken, which included a bottle of wine between us at lunch. I made the excuse I was going to catch a train and left the hotel at 5pm, going across the road to the park, where I must have dozed off as it was about quarter to six when I got back to the hotel. Before I went to the hotel, I got my bag from the station cloakroom. I walked back into the hotel and the manager asked me if I had fallen asleep and missed my train – I answered 'Yes'. I then had a wash and brush up and went to have some dinner. The same waitress served me as at lunchtime.

I left the hotel between 6.30pm and 6.45pm and booked a ticket to Leeds, 3rd class. The train was due to go after 7pm and I had a long conversation with the ticket collector, which lasted ten to fifteen minutes. I got on the train and had to change at Stretford. I arrived at Leeds after midnight and went to the Metropole. Leaving my bag there. I went to the Nursing Home but didn't see Nora – I saw the Night Sister."

Supt Spooner, I said. "All this information needs to be verified, and if it pans out, then Green would have an alibi for the time of the murder."

"Ah but, from what I can see there is still the vital period between 5pm and 5.45pm for which he claimed to have dozed off on the park bench."

Seeing Green again, Supt Spooner asked him. "So, Green, Supt Lockley tells me you received two rings from your friends, Lorenzo and Charlie. This was in Leeds."

"Yes, that's right. I'd been out of work since 1st July and was getting stuck for money – could'nt thoil owt (*couldn't afford anything*)."

"I hear from Nora Lammey that you were going under the name of Terry Green. Is that correct?"

At the mention of this name, Leslie Green seemed to change slightly, he closed his eyes and his expression went blank. Then he was back again. This may have been circumstantial but Supt Spooner noticed a significant chance in his stance, more relaxed than the straight-backed army stance of Leslie Green. Green got out his comb and combed his hair, then brushed down and straightened his suit. There was also a significant change in the way he spoke – more clipped, with a degree of authority in his voice. Gone was the Yorkshire brogue.

Yes, I had told Nora Lammey that my name was Terry, not Leslie. Leslie, I would say, is rather lame. Now Terry, Terry has power, leadership qualities, don't you think Superintendent Spooner?"

"I don't know, Green. You tell me."

The story played out……….

I met Nora at a dance in Leeds, the last week in April. I loved the soft lilt of her Irish accent and she was pleasant-looking, pretty in fact, so I took a fancy to her. I asked her for a dance. They were playing a slow one, "Please Mr Sun, by Johnnie Ray."

"Let's sit down," I suggested. So we sat and introduced ourselves and got talking.

"I'm Terry… Terry Green. I'm actually in Leeds on business, just thought I'd take some time off and come to this dance."

Nora replied, "I'm working as a nurse, at the Claremont Nursing Home, here in Leeds."

So, we had a few dances. The music was good, with Rosemary Clooney singing "Botch-a-Me my baby, a really fun song, getting everyone up dancing.

Most of the other songs around were slow, romantic ones so great for romantic twosome close-dancing to songs like 'Tell me Why' by the Four Aces, 'Walking my baby back home', another one by Johnnie Ray – he had three songs being played regularly including 'Cry'. He was so well liked, with his soulful sort of cry in his voice. This was followed by "Trying to forget you' by the Hillstoppers.

(What I, Leslie actually remember about this was a bit hazy. I seemed to be looking at Nora through my eyes, but I wasn't speaking to her. My mouth was moving, but I wasn't saying the words that came out. It was a very strange feeling. I felt remote, cut off, not part of the conversation. Then I had a voice in my head that said to me, "There Leslie, I've done the introductions. She's nice isn't she? Go on, take your chance, get to know her. Forget about the family, they're history. Nora doesn't need to know the truth, just keep reality out of it." Then, all of a sudden I was there, with Nora in front of me. I stammered a bit, but managed to carry on the conversation.)

The dance ended with 'High Noon' by Frankie Laine to which we all started singing… 'Do not forsake me oh my darling…".

We started going out together. After the first meeting we met almost every weekend. Most of the time I was 'listening in' while this other voice spoke. "I'm a nephew of Mr Wiltshaw, a renowned pottery manufacturer in Stoke, and I work for him as a traveller connected with the pottery business. Actually, I get to travel all over the place, London, Somerset, Birmingham, and even New York." (I, Leslie, took part in some of the meetings, but mostly in the background, looking on, but listening. This voice in my head seemed to know what to say and how to act. So I let it, as I was a shy sort of fellow, although my head would clear sometimes so that I found myself able to interact.)

So I, as Terry Green, whenever possible, would 'borrow' the Wiltshaws' car for jaunts in which I posed as a man of means. The high-priced car, my immaculate appearance, courteous behaviour and well-modulated voice led people to believe that I was what I gave myself out to be, and I loved it.

On May 2, I visited Leeds in Mr Wiltshaw's Rover car. Of course, I told Nora that the car was mine. I took her to a medical ball in Leeds. She loved the car.

Nora took her annual holiday from 23rd June to 9th July, going home to Ballymena, in Northern Ireland.

"I visited her twice, taking a plane over, the only way to travel, don't you think Superintendent Spooner?"

I didn't wait for an answer. It all had to end though. Mr Wiltshaw had had enough of me taking the car for my own use, and had dismissed me. I managed to find bits and pieces of work, but that all dried up by 1st July and I was feeling the pinch, money-wise. There was no way I could keep up this pretence with no money, especially having taken two plane crossings to Ireland with Nora.

On the second visit, I proposed. Nora was all excited but added, "Terry, we hardly know anything about each other."
"I know, but if you feel the same about me as I feel about you, I think we should get married. Getting to know each other will take time, and I don't want to wait. I wouldn't have come all the way over here if I didn't love you. Now, what do you say?"

So we agreed we were going to get married and went to see about getting a marriage certificate.

"I do not want you to carry on working, Nora. What would you think if I told you to leave your job on 21st July so we can marry soon after?"

So, that was settled.

On 9th July we both returned by air to Leeds. I was signing the hotel register as Mr Wiltshaw, whenever I stayed. I stayed there on July 11th to 13th, about three days before the murder.

I loved the idea of people thinking I had money and looking up to me. I had always dreamed that one day I would be rich and be more than just a driver, someone of means and quality and I was going to do it, by hook or by crook. I could imitate Mr Wilshaw fairly well, the way he talked and the way he held himself. He had an air about him, that showed to the world he was important and a man to be reckoned with. I was going to show the world I was important too. But, how was I going to do that if I had no money. So I asked a man I knew if he could loan me something.

"No way, pal. Go and ask some other stooge." So, I had no luck there.

Nora had lent me a small amount of money in Ireland as I said I had not brought enough with me. She lent me £8.

Nora later gave me the spare cash she had, just £5, but it wasn't enough.

I was in desperate straits for money. I went back again to the man I tried to borrow money from before.

"Look, I desperately need money, at least £20. Can you just help out a friend, please. I've got the hotel bill to pay."

"As I said before, I know your type. You're just a swindler. You've got nothing to fall back on, so how are you going to pay me back, hmm? No way, sorry pal."

I returned to the hotel, to the reception.
.
"Sorry to inconvenience you, but I have had my raincoat stolen, which had my wallet in the pocket. I would like to report its theft. I find myself without any ready cash at present. I know it's an awful thing to ask, but would there be any way you would allow my bill to stand over for a few days until I can get back to Stoke. It will

87

only be a few days, then I can pay the hotel in full. You know I have the money, just not on me."

"By all means, Mr Wiltshaw. I am sure that can be arranged." So, I had breathing space.

It was now July 13th. "Nora, unfortunately it looks like my raincoat and wallet have been stolen. I have reported the theft to the reception at the hotel but I find myself, temporarily, lacking in cash. I hate to ask this again but, do you think you could lend me something for the time being? I need the train fare to Stoke-on-Trent. Don't worry, I will be back on 16th or 17th July, and will pay you everything back."

In the early morning of July 14th I left Leeds for London and stayed at the Strand Palace Hotel. While I was there I wrote, in the name of Wiltshaw, asking for accommodation to be reserved for me at the Hotel Metropole on July 17.

("So, he didn't return to Stoke" Spooner thought to himself.)

I managed to steel a few wallets while I was in London.

On 16th July, I got myself rather pissed in the Stafford Hotel. I was going to go back to Leeds, but I sat down on a park bench, and just nodded off.

So, on 17th July I returned and called for Nora at the nursing home, about 9pm. We had some drinks together at the Metropole Hotel. That is when I gave her two rings.

We went for tea at her friend's flat, a Miss Greta Davies, also a nurse - that was 18th July. We got talking. That's when I said, "I'm sorry, but I can't stay long. I've just heard that my aunt, Mrs

Wiltshaw, has been brutally attacked with an old-fashioned poker. In all accounts it was a very brutal murder."

"That's awful sorry to hear, Terry, how sad for your uncle." Nora replied.

"Yes, as soon as I heard the news, I drove down to Stone, in Staffordshire, to visit my uncle. I hired a car this time, not having the Rover here. I told him I had to get back to see you and tell you the news and uncle said that I had to hurry back as they were roping everyone in, anyone who knew my aunt. So, I have to go. Sorry for the short visit."

"That's no problem," Greta replied, "just hope they catch the bugger soon. Oh, he should be locked away and lose the key, or even hang him, for a crime such as that!"

On July 18 Nora received a letter from her sister in Belfast.
"The police have been to see my sister in Belfast, Terry." Nora said, "They are looking for a man called Leslie Green for the murder of your aunt."

"Oh, don't be silly Nora, there are loads of people with the surname Green. I am not involved. Someone with a similar name has murdered my aunt, that's all there is to it."

"I don't know, Terry. I'm not happy with police going all the way over to Ireland to see my sister. There's got to be something you're not telling me. Here." and she reached into her handbag, "I don't want them." and handed me the two rings. "Until this murder is sorted out, I'm not marrying you."

"Ok, if you wish, just to calm your nerves, I will return to Staffordshire and try to sort this out." Nora seemed to be happy with that.

89

I had got cases for the rings but, as Nora didn't want them we'd gone for a walk beside the canal, in Park Square Gardens, Leeds, and sat on a bench. I threw the two rings away, with the boxes, in the canal at Leeds.

…………………..

Finishing my story, Supt Spooner then showed me a map, "I want you to indicate with a cross exactly where you threw the rings.

So, I marked a cross on the map.

Also, the police physician mentioned you had a cut on the inside of your wrist. Can you tell me how you got that?"

"I think it must have been Monday, 14th July, in the afternoon of that day. I did it when I fell down the steps at Ilkley Moor – I grazed my wrist on one of the stone steps. I didn't think it was bad enough to see a doctor. I was on my own at the time, just out walking. It was a lovely day, with the sun out, so I was in my shirt sleeves."

Looking at the medical report again, Supt Spooner stated, "Our physician also found a cut on your left thumb. Do you remember how you came about that cut?"

"Well, you know Nora and I were courting and we'd stayed out late. I wasn't allowed into the nurses' quarters at night but, well, when we got back to the nurses quarters, the doors were locked and Nora couldn't get back in. So, I tried a window. There were roses growing around it. That's probably where I got the scratches. I managed to open the window and crawl through, intending to go in and open the door for Nora, but there was a nail sticking out of the window frame, and I caught my thumb on it. I remember it bled quite a bit."

"Hmm. OK, Green. That's all for now."

Chapter 13

Spooner and Lockley discussed this interview afterwards.

"You're right, Lockley, he's a strange man. He's got the knack of imitating Mr Wiltshaw down to a tea – can put on airs and graces if he wants to. Anyway, he indicated on this map where he threw the two rings into the canal, so I'll arrange for Leeds police to do a search and dredge the canal, if need be."

Supt Spooner got the map delivered to Leeds police and also arranged a search of Nurse Davies' apartment in Belmont Grove, Leeds. Detective Officer Cairns carried out that search, eventually finding a gold chain in a cavity in an inside coal house. The cavity was about 8 feet off the ground. When he pulled the chain out, he saw that two rings were attached to it. Nothing else was found in the apartment, following a thorough search. A search was also carried out at the Hotel Metropole by police officers, but nothing was found.

……..

So, I was back in my cell. That meeting with Spooner was a bit of a haze. What had I actually said to him? Maybe it was just the tension of the situation. Things were getting nowhere fast. What the hell were these policemen doing all this time? I was left in the dark. Again, I started to think that they were trying to find some evidence to plant on me. Maybe I should have asked for legal aid, but so far, I'd only been charged with larceny.

I started thinking of Nora to take my mind off the murder charge. We just clicked and she bought out the best in me – stopped me being in the doldrums. She also loved it when my voice changed to that of a toff. She would laugh and say, "Say something to me in your posh voice, Terry." So, Terry would come through and speak on my behalf, "I just spent £300 on a limousine and discovered that the fee does not include a driver. I cannot believe I have spent all that money and have nothing to chauffeur it!" It took her a second or two then had a fit of giggles. "That's a good yun, Terry." And gave me a kiss and a hug.

She was so different from Constance. Constance was fine first of all – I had some much-needed stability in my life, especially when baby Gillian was born. Then with all the worries about me keeping jobs, even though I was providing for them, she started nagging. She wanted a house, with a mortgage. I couldn't provide suitable proof to the bank that I was receiving a guaranteed wage, so Constance had to get a job, which meant relying on her nag of a mother for baby-sitting duties. I couldn't be doing with the rows, so I'd go off for days at a time, doing my own thing.

I was falling for Nora. There was nothing I could do about it. I didn't want to lose her, so the lies continued. I proposed to Nora and she was so thrilled, although I never told her I was already married and would have to seek a divorce. That was wicked of me, but I just loved seeing her happy and hearing her bubbly laughter. We had all sorts of plans. This voice in my head that spoke with the posh accent told her, through me, that he would buy her a little cottage – I don't know why, I think he just wanted that. He wanted the good things in life and I suppose she just was so joyful when he talked of things like that. I knew I couldn't afford it and could never buy her a cottage, but I found myself going along with it, just caught up in the moment, I suppose.

Talking about the cottage and their future marriage, Terry told Nora another joke:

"A young couple about to be married were looking over a house in the country. After satisfying themselves that it was suitable they started for home. During the return journey the young lady was seemingly absorbed in deep thought, and being asked the reason for her silence, she asked the question: 'Did you notice a W.C. at the house?' The young man, not having noticed any, ultimately wrote to the landlord inquiring where it was situated. The landlord did not understand what a 'W.C.' meant and, after thinking it over for some time came to the conclusion that it meant 'Wesleyan Church'. He replied as follows:

'I very much regret the delay in replying to your letter, but I have the pleasure of informing you that the W.C is situated 9 miles from the house and is capable of seating 260 people. This is very unfortunate for you if you are in the habit of going regularly, but no doubt you will be glad to know that a great many people take their lunch with them and make a day of it. Others, who cannot spare the time, go by car, arriving just in time, but generally they are in such a hurry they cannot wait. The last time my wife and I went was six years ago and we had to stand all the time. It may interest you to know that a bazaar is to be given in order to furnish the W.C. with plush seats, as the members feel that it is a long-felt want. I might mention that it pains us not to be able to go more often.'"

Well we both creased up with laughter. "I love you Terry Green" Nora replied through her laughter. "And I love you too Nora."

Those were good memories.

Chapter 14

Those good memories didn't last though. They were based on fiction, although Nora had stuck by me, even after finding out who I really was and all the lies I'd told her. She was real, flesh and bone and she loved me. Would I ever get out of here and see her again? I so much wanted to see her again, to start afresh, get myself a job and get her that cottage.

Probably with the stress of it all, I found myself back into my war memories again.

……………..

 By December 1941 I was back in Leeds, on leave, going back to see mum and my little sister. Everywhere was a wreck, the place had been repeatedly bombed with the shattered walls of buildings I once knew and had passed by regularly or even entered - steel pulled out of shape as though it were plasticine, making weird forms amongst the broken bricks and shattered glass strewn around. I took a walk around. Leeds New Station had been hit; the Town Hall, which included the Law Library, had been peppered with shrapnel. The city's museum on Park Row; the Kirkgate Markets; the Central Post Office; the Quarry Hill flats and the Hotel Metropole. Thousands of houses had also been destroyed. The Museum's beautiful facade that had been built in 1821, looked like it was in the process of being dismantled. Aire Street had been basically flattened. Kirkstall power station had been a target. The Hepworth Arcade and the streets around Water

Lane were burnt out; Mill Hill Chapel, the Royal Exchange Building, Denby & Spink's furniture store and the Yorkshire Post building had all been hit.

I hadn't heard of Leeds being bombed. Glasgow had taken a right hammering, but we just heard of 'a Northern town' being bombed just after 9 pm on Friday 14 March 1941. I got talking to a guy while waiting for a train. He told me that around 40 bombers took part in the raid on Leeds. Incendiary bombs were first dropped onto the city on the Friday night, later high explosive bombs were dropped on the Saturday. A total of 25 tons of bombs fell on Leeds during the raid.

I got the train to Middleton. There was no-one in and it looked like there hadn't been anyone there for some time. I stood there for a bit. I was getting anxious just looking at the building which held so many bad memories for me. I decided to knock at nextdoor's, which was answered by the elderly gentleman living there. "I'm sorry son, your mum and your sister were staying with your uncle that night. They'd been theer for some time, as yer mum was finding it difficult to cope and she dint want the little girl taken away from her. I haven't heard anything since. Sorry, I can't 'elp yer."

I thanked him. I knew where they might have gone and made my way to Hunslett Carr.

I found myself standing across from a burned out building. Half of the semi-detached building had crumbled into a mass of stone, brick and glass. The other half was burnt black. I could see traces of the wallpaper on the remaining joining wall, with broken furniture, kitchen bits and pieces, beds, just peeping sadly and dejected through the rubble. I sat down on what remained of the old front garden wall, and found myself crying.

Someone approached me. "Nah then, you must be Leslie, the son. Yer ma and little sister and yer uncle dint stand a chance. The bombs just came darn and then theer was nowt left.

I managed to stammer out, "Wh…why did no-one tell me?"

…………………

I was lost. Nowhere to go. I'd come back to see mum as she'd got a bit better with me over the years and was proud of my joining the army and, basically, I had nowhere else to go. All my family were gone now. Where did I belong? My head started aching again. I should have made my way back to Middleton, at least I could have somewhere to stay and a change of clothes, but I wasn't thinking straight and, in any case, I didn't want to stay there, with so many memories, most of them nasty – that cupboard under the stairs, the thrashings, the insults, the rape, made to feel I was worthless! All of those memories started flashing before me. I couldn't stand it. I had to get away.

I don't know what happened then, but I found myself back at Leeds Station again. I felt strange again, as though I wasn't in control of my actions anymore.

I don't know why I did it, impulse I suppose, but saw a man deposit a suitcase at his feet. He was about the same size as me. I needed a change of clothes and thought there might be something else of interest, even money, in the suitcase. Something I could flog. This other person, using my body, picked his chance and slipped round the back of him, deftly picking up the suitcase as he/I passed by. Trouble is, he couldn't have realised how heavy the suitcase was. There was no way I could run with it and, anyway, that would have given me away immediately – seeing someone running with a suitcase.

Anyway, the shout went up, "Thief, thief", with people looking astounded in my direction.

Station police were on me in a couple of seconds.

Leeds Magistrates sentenced me to six months on 6th December 1941.

In 1943 we were stationed in Bath. I was sent to Borstal for training.

....

I married Constance on 18 May 1945. We met at a dance and got on well. I needed some sort of stability in my life and Constance provided that. Then, the following year, Gillian was born. I was still in the army though, so we hardly saw each other. Constance stayed with her parents in Stoke-on-Trent.

I was lucky in that my regiment stayed in the UK, as a defence unit. The war was declared over, but I stayed with the army.

Then, the unit was sent to Trieste. We were in a small town called Opinica, which sat on the top of a hill overlooking the Bay of Trieste. The view from the peak was so picturesque. The area was known as the Morgan Line and acted as a buffer zone between the Yugoslavs and the Italians, both of whom laid claim to this territory. The barracks we moved into had formerly belonged to an Italian army unit and were quite spacious.

The regiment was very involved with the keeping of the peace in Trieste itself, as there were a lot of political parties and even numerous states trying to seize control of the Venezia Giulia area. It was quite common to be sitting in a cinema in town and to have a notice flashed on the screen that said: 'All troops must return immediately to their units.'

On our arrival back in camp we would find ourselves being armed and sent back to the town in convoy to control the riots that were taking place.

The system for release from the army at that time was based on a combination of age and length of service. This then gave you a 'group number', and over the next year or so each group number came up in turn and the members of that group received their discharge. The lower the group number the quicker you got out. My own group number was 48, rather high because I was only 16 when I was called up.

While we were stationed here I got my first leave home back to England, so got to see Constance and baby Gillian.

In 1949, back in Trieste after my leave I found that the riots were still in full swing and that many more of the older and longer-serving members having left, including some of my friends. I wanted to go home and living in fear of being involved in a situation that might postpone my home posting.

I saw my chance. There was a lot of black-marketing going on and the Yugloslavs wanted army truck tyres. They were worth quite a bit and, if I could get them to the Yugloslavs, maybe I could afford to buy myself out of the army. As luck would have it, there was a jeep free, near a hoist, and I hoisted these tyres onto the back of the jeep. I was seen, nonetheless - the young assistant of the Tech Corporal in charge of Squadron Technical Stores, reported me.

I was brought back from Trieste for theft. I got 12 months, after which I was discharged from the army.

So, I was free! But I needed a job and the only thing I was fit for was driving, so got lots of driving jobs. I'd got numerous jobs – insurance man, bread driver, barman, bouncer but nothing really stuck – I suppose they just weren't interesting and I found myself out on my ear most of the time.

In February 1950 I worked, for a short time, as an attendant at the Cameo ballroom, in Longton, Stoke, above Burton's the tailors. The atmosphere was great – everyone mixing and having good times… good music. Décor was not so good though, very rough around the edges – naked light bulbs, bare boards and flaking paintwork with a sad string of fairy lights to add a bit of faded glamour. There was a big window in the ladies' loo, so I was told, with clear glass in it, so lucky they were upstairs.

People were ink-stamped on their hands when they paid to come in, so they could come and go as they wished.

The Ceramic City Stompers visited every so often, although they mainly played at the Embassy Ballroom in Burslem. The stompers were rough but ready jazz players. Rash young ladies would send them letters. Jazz had taken over from Jive and Swing of the war years. The Smokey City Jazzmen were around at the time too, playing trumpet, double bass, drums, clarinet, piano and trombone. People loved "If I were a Bell" from the musical Guys and Dolls, the music of Humphrey Littleton "I play as I please". Cool Jazz had also come in, introducing a calmer, smoother sound and linear melodic lines, "Get your Kicks on Route 66" and "Nature Boy" by Nat King Cole and "Night Train" by Jimmy Forest.

The place was heaving on a Saturday night. That's when I met Lorenzo. Lorenzo approached me there and said he remembered that they were in the same cell some years ago. Lorenzo was a bit light-fingered too. So, we became good friends. The Cameo was an alcohol-free establishment but every so often someone would try to spoil the night by bringing in alcohol and topping up his orange juice. One night, I was asked to throw a drunk out and Lorenzo came to my assistance. He was throwing punches, one of which hit me square in the face. I don't remember much then, just seeing the guy at the bottom of the stairs, obviously with a broken arm.

Lorenzo was looking astonished. "You learnt that in the army did you?"
"What do yer mean? I didn't do anything. He tripped didn't he?" Looking down at him, I said, "His arm's twisted, probably broken - must have done that in the fall."

Lorenzo didn't seem to mind that the drunk had been hurt, but was still looking at me as though I'd lost my marbles. "Oh well, serves him right." He eventually said.

I overheard him speaking to Charlie another time. "Be wary of that Leslie, he can change just like that." and he clicked his fingers. That time I told you he threw that drunk down the stairs, well a strange, menacing look came over his face, a sort of a snarl, something I wouldn't like to witness again, then Leslie grabbed the guy's arm, twisted it round the back of him, then outwards. I heard the crack and the guy screamed. Leslie then stuck his leg out and pushed him backwards, seeing him tumble down the stairs."

"You two talking about me agin." I said
"Just about that drunk incident at the Cameo." Charlie replied
"Yer, silly bugger went and tripped himself he was so sozzled, then fell down the stairs, breaking his arm."

Both Charlie and Lorenzo looked away and carried on with what they were doing but they seemed to be a bit cagy with me afterwards, which I never understood. I mean, he did trip himself up and break his arm in the fall, so what had I done wrong?

Anyway, we had good times with good music at the Cameo. There was a young lady there taking the coats. I quite fancied her and would chat her up, but she wouldn't have anything to do with me as she knew I was married. At the time I was living in Beeston Street and working as an insurance man during the week. I used to go to a young girl's house at Sandford Hill Farm in the late 40s, maybe early 50s until she too found out I was married. This girl started working taking coats at the Cameo a bit later, after I'd left.

At any rate, I finally got the job with the Wiltshaws in October 1950. While in the Army I had continued improving my knowledge of motor-vehicles – how to take an engine apart and put it together again - and this must have helped me get the job as chauffeur/handyman with the Wiltshaws. Constance was pleased for me, some stability in my life for once, and we now had a place of our own, although had to pay the mortgage. It was alright for a time, but this voice in my head kept telling me I wanted more and that I wasn't really happy doing what I was doing. The voice told me I wanted that recognition I felt when I'd worn the Canadian Corporal's uniform, with the stripes and emblems – a feeling, no matter how brief, of being respected.

Chapter 15

After a three-day session in Stafford, I was committed to Stafford Assizes to undertake trial on a charge of murdering Mrs Alice Maud Mary Wiltshaw, of Estoril, Barlaston, near Stafford, wife of a pottery manufacturer.

The map was handed in by Superintendent Spooner as an exhibit in the case.

Terry had decided to wear a light tweed suit, a yellow shirt and a maroon tie with white spots. "Yes, that will do. I think I look quite dapper – ready to meet my audience." I was escorted into the Courtroom on Wednesday, August 6, 1952 by two police officers. I smiled at the huge crowd of people collected there in the gallery. I wanted to give the impression that I was confident that these charges against Leslie were made up.

The charge was read out that I had wilfully murdered Mrs Alice Maud Mary Wiltshaw, aged 62, of Barlaston, on July 16th.

The Clerk, Mr A E Tritschler, asked me if I understood the charge. I answered in a firm clear voice, "Yes, sir".

He asked me if I wished to add anything, which I declined.

The Clerk then stated, "The last time you were here, I asked you if you wished to be represented and you declined. You may think well about that now. Do you want legal aid?"

As I was now on a murder charge, I felt I wanted somebody to represent me, to tell my story to the courtroom, and I answered:

"Yes, sir."

At that point superintendent W Crook spoke, "I wish to ask for a remand in custody for the prisoner, until next Wednesday. By then, I hope to be able to say when the case will be able to proceed."

The Magistrate, Mr R F Goodill granted the remand in custody and legal aid.

So, the following Wednesday came (August 13th). I appeared at Stone Court again, on the charge of murdering Mrs Wiltshaw. I'd dressed myself smartly again and again smiled, walking briskly to the dock, where I sat down. I thought we'd be getting on with the case and was tensed up, wondering what lies they would have thought up and I was perplexed that no reference was made to the larceny charges during the proceedings, apart from the Magistrate stating that they were to be entered on the Court sheet for the day, but then again, I thought, what was the point of investigating larceny charges when they could get me for murder?

I was remanded yet again for a further seven days.

I was asked by the Clerk if I had anything to say. I again replied, "No, sir."

Superintendent W Crook had been the one to ask for the remand, and I overheard him saying to the Magistrate that Chief Superintendent Tom Lockley, head of Staffordshire C.I.D. had gone to London to confer with the Director of Public Prosecutions and arrange a suitable day when the case could be heard.

Chapter 16

Superintendent T Bowman, Head of Leeds I.D. and I, Superintendent Spooner, were making investigations in Leeds while Green had been remanded. Of course, the local newspapers were hot on my heels, trying to ascertain what progress we had made in our investigations into the murder. I advised Supt Bowman just to advise The Yorkshire Post that I am here on routine inquiries.

Of course, the reporters weren't just in Leeds but were harassing Chief Det. Super T Lockley. He spoke to the Yorkshire Evening Post on Wednesday, 20 August, saying, "The papers in the case are now in the hands of the Director of Public Prosecutions. Within two or three days, it should be possible to consult the Court about a date for the preliminary Hearing."

While Supt Bowman and I (Spooner) were in Leeds was getting feedback from the Leeds detectives, who had searched the room that Green had occupied at the Hotel Metropole. Even water cisterns in the hotel were emptied and examined, but without success.

After Green had told the police that he had thrown some ring cases in the river from the bridge near the Golden Lion Hotel, Leeds, I decided to do a bit of a survey. One Sunday morning, while few people were about, I dropped ring cases in the River Aire to see what happened to them. In a boat below the bridge, Leeds police officers watched as the ring boxes floated down river.

Afterwards, undergrowth on the banks was searched, but no trace of the missing boxes was found. So, that seemed to be a dead end too. However, some days later, a Leeds Corporation gardener, Jack Higgins, called on 30th July to say that he had found two ring cases in an iris bed in Park Square Gardens, where Green had sat with Miss Nora Lammey,

....

By the time I (Leslie) had been called back to the bench after a fourth remand, I was getting quite angry. I asked to speak to the defending solicitor, who had been appointed to me, Mr G G Baker, QC, asking what was happening.

"If they havna got enough information on me to make a case, they can't keep me on remand. It's unfair. I'm stuck here like a caged animal and I want you to tell them either to get their act together or let me go."

"Yes, it is an unconventional way of going about things and I can quite understand your displeasure. I will convey your message and see where it gets us."

Mr Baker returned to visit me. "Mr R D Goodwill, chairman of Stone Magistrates, has put our views forward to the Director of Public Prosecutions, He emphatically put your case forward, saying that the delay is unfair to you, the accused, adding that he thinks it is about time that this case should proceed, in all fairness to the prisoner, as you have now been in custody for over a month."

"So, have you heard anything further?"

"Unfortunately, you are to be remanded for yet another week, at the request of Superintendent Crook. I understanding the dates September 8, 9, 11 and 12 have been mentioned by the Director of Prosecutions as likely dates for the preliminary Hearing.

106

"Oh, that's just ridiculous!" and I banged the table and started strutting around the room, pulling at my hair. The room was going dizzy.

I saw a look of horror come across Mr Baker and he took a few steps back towards the door.

This gruff voice came out of me, growling. "Gerrout, sling yer hook, yer lying scum." it screamed.

The dizziness went but left me still so pissed off. Trying to get control again I managed to continue, calmer, "What made-up charges are they trying to pin on me?" I didna do it. I wasna theer. They've got no-one else so they want to fabricate the truth. Maybe they've found some of the jewellery and have planted it in places I've been, just to make me look guilty?"

Mr Baker replied, rather hesitantly, "I am sure that is not the case but, obviously, I can see your frustration. Unfortunately, it is out of my hands. I cannot hasten the proceedings."

Mr Baker hurried out and spoke to the guard, "Did you see that? His face physically changed – there was definitely what I can only say looked like a demonic look his eyes – only for a second or two but sure made the hair on the back of my neck stand up – and I'm supposed to defend that! I'm going to arrange for the psychiatrist to look in on him."

An examination into Green's mental state was carried out by the Principal Medical Officer of Holloway Prison, Dr Thomas Christie. I tried to answer his questions to the best of my ability. He did ask me about voices in my head telling me to commit murder, but there was no way I was going to reply in the affirmative, even though it was brought to my attention that, if it was proved I had a mental illness, I could not be hanged for the murder. In my mind, I felt such a thing was an excuse that prisoners used to get out of murder charges – make up stories that they were hearing voices telling them to kill. I hadn't committed the murder and I didn't want to admit to hearing voices. My voices were not telling me to kill, so I just denied hearing voices. It wasn't what this doctor wanted to hear and I didn't want a mental illness tag for the rest of my life. He did ask me about feeling a degree of anger that I could not control. I stated that I had no memories of ever being in a situation where I felt out of control and could not control my anger.

Christie's report stated, "He is an intelligent man of the soldierly type, smart, alert, quick to understand and reply to questions and capable of sustaining conversation in a relevant manner. His general bearing is that of a trained soldier and there is nothing in his appearance or conduct to suggest mental abnormality."

So much for that, but those tests were just run of the mill – ask a few questions, get them right, and you're deemed fit.

Chapter 17

TERRY

Leslie was asleep, sleeping fitfully. I rose. Of course, Leslie rose with me so I couldn't look down on his sleeping body.

"That Leslie had got himself in a right pickle now." I said to myself. "The poor thing. He was never all that bright." I'd been taking over intermittently ever since he was a child and locked in that cupboard under the stairs. He had become so stressed – psychotic I would say. That's when I came about, Terry. I was the one who got him out of stressful situations, when he just couldn't cope anymore and was reduced to a crying lump of intense fear of helplessness. I would take on the stress and pain. I made him go to sleep and I stepped up to the spot – that means that I took over the consciousness while Terrance and Leslie faded into the background and slept. It was me, Terry, who had gone to school that week and performed so well in the maths test. It was me who carried his hurt, when he was raped repeatedly by his uncle. It was me who took over for a year at school, after he had been beaten and almost suffocated by the street gang. Of course, this left Leslie completely bewildered. He didn't know I existed. All he knew was that he had 'lost' seven days first of all, then had lost a whole year – a year he had no recollection of. Of course, poor Leslie was still traumatised – he still had the initial memories of an assault but no memories after that. I had to keep him asleep until I felt he was mentally stable enough to return. I couldn't have him trying to kill himself, otherwise that would be the end of me too. He had made attempts on numerous occasions, being so overwhelmed with depression, that he was incapable of self-comfort or finding a way to put his trauma behind him and get on with life. Poor Leslie had no-one to turn to, no-one to discuss his inadequacies, his abandonment, his intense feelings of rejection, especially since his mother turned from him. But, of course, being asleep, Leslie had no memories of what had happened during the 'lost time'.

Leslie started to make up stories to cover the time loss. Some were believable, if you didn't check them out, but the thing is, he just wasn't any good at making things up. He wasn't even any good at making up fairy stories to tell to little Gillian, as most parents are.

Actually, he wasn't good at much. He could drive, yes, but he couldn't hold down a job. I suppose that might have had something to do with me as I got bored and wanted to be elsewhere, such as the races. So, Leslie didn't turn up regularly and couldn't be relied on.

It wouldn't have been so bad if Leslie had any get up and go – out finding a good job where he'd make a bit of money and could improve his lifestyle. No, but there he was, stuck in a rut, pinching the odd wallet or two to keep the family ticking over.

I suppose I was the being that Leslie could have been if he'd been given a chance. I wanted to see the sights – go to London, go to a show, get a nice car, go on holiday, go abroad even. I wanted to be something – someone people respected and looked up to, but no, he kept me there in boring local driving jobs, delivering bread or such like.

Well, I wasn't going to have it much longer and I saw my chance when Leslie got the job as chauffeur for the Wiltshaws. I loved their Rover car – so expensive, chic and comfortable - a fashion symbol. People looked as we drove by. I wanted that car.

I took over from Leslie some weekends and would drive. Of course Mr Wiltshaw didn't know that Leslie had 'borrowed' the car. That's when I ended up in Leeds one day, going originally to the racetrack at Wetherby but heard of a dance going on and thought that would be fun.

It was there, at the dance, that I met Nora Lammey, a sweet little Irish girl. I could tell that Leslie liked her too but he wasn't going to approach her because he had a wife and child, so I did. I mean, I wasn't married with a child – I could do what I wanted and I wanted Nora. I let Leslie into our conversations – I spoke through him, giving him the words to say, and let him actually take over sometimes. He needed a bit of romance in his life and a bit of make-believe and he was enjoying himself. He didn't seem to mind Nora calling him Terry – it didn't worry him as numerous people had called him Terrance or Terry over the years.

I told her (through Leslie), that I was rich, and the car was mine. I even booked into the Metropole Hotel in Leeds under the name of Terry Wiltshaw. I was a good mimic and could take him off to a tee – well spoken, well dressed, diplomatic. Well, you know all that. I'd chosen Leslie's clothes. He'd prefer baggy trousers and a shirt and jumper, but I wanted to be dapper, with tailored trousers, jacket and tie, fashionable for a young man at the time. I looked the part.

Then Leslie lost his job with the Wiltshaws for taking the car too many times – my fault I admit. So, I had no money coming in and I needed money to keep up that lifestyle.

Leslie couldn't get another job, his reputation had gone before him. So I was stuck.

I went down to London. Leslie knew he was there, vaguely, but didn't know why or what he did. I was on the rob - wallets mainly. I took a train to Ascot, to the races, there was always good picking there. The people who won were always over the moon and not paying much attention to where they pocketed their money as they were so excited. Some even dropped notes as they went, with their pockets stuffed – easy picking.

Of course, when Leslie was interrogated by the police, all he could say that he went to London and walked about looking at the shops. As I said, he was never great at making up stories. I mean, who goes to London to look at the shops and not have the money to buy anything? Yes, we did stay at the Strand Palace Hotel and, when Leslie took over again, he had money in his pockets that he did not know how he got. Anyway, Leslie now had money to pay the bill at the Metropole. I wrote from the Strand Palace Hotel to the Metropole Hotel, asking for a room to be booked for me for 17th July.

There wasn't just me and Leslie though, occupying the same body. I knew about Terrance. Leslie had no idea why he got himself into so much trouble during the war years. He had no memory of events leading up to him being arrested. I tried to keep Terrance under control but it wasn't always possible because he was a law until himself. Terrance only appeared when a situation called for anger or defence, when Leslie got really riled or was under attack. Terrance was there to protect Leslie.

Terrance did appear for an instant when Leslie was young and was angry about his father's treatment of him, so he started trying to kill birds in the yard.

The next time Terrance appeared was at borstal when someone was taunting Leslie, calling him names. Leslie would have just taken it on the chin, little frightened squirt that he is, but Terrance was having nothing of it. Terrance got angry and knocked him out. Of course, Leslie got put into the hell hole to calm down.

The next we hear of Terrance is in the evacuation from Dunkirk. Leslie was scared out of his skin, and who can blame him,

112

everyone was. He hid his head in the sand while the bombs and guns were blasting overhead and landing inches away from him.

Terrance wasn't having that – he had to save Leslie, and himself. He got himself out back into the water to try and get on one of the many ships taking them all back to Blightie. But, as those ships were sunk, one by one, all hope was failing. Terrance was out of his depth too, quite literally in the water, he couldn't just punch out to get out of this situation but he had to save himself.

Men were starting to queue for boats. I had to laugh, queuing, of all things – so totally British! We were all having to wade back out to the boats, many of us waiting hours in shoulder-deep water.

The planes were shooting at us. We were all sitting targets. Terrance raised his rifle and shot back, over and over, then felt myself being grabbed by the shoulders, "Don't be a fool, do you want to attract more fire to us? You can't do anything to protect us with a rifle."

So, seeing sense, Terrance grudgingly waited in the queue, soaked and freezing, hungry, scared and totally incapable of doing anything to protect ourselves, with nowhere to hide.

Only the wounded were got away that night. We were all at our lowest, our nerves at breaking-point. Sleep was impossible. We just had to wait, wait, wait, chest-deep in water. No-one knew if the ships were coming back for us, just waiting for the onslaught of bombing to begin again.

In the early hours, HMS Wakeful, full with evacuated British soldiers, was torpedoed and the ship broke into pieces. We saw HMS Grafton approaching, only to be torpedoed by a U-boat. Worse was to come with HMS Lydd, mistaking Comfort, a British drifter, for a German vessel, slammed into it, cutting the drifter in half, killing nearly everyone on board.

One by one the Luftwaffe attacked the ships trying to take us back. Men were crying, being comforted by other shell-shocked men.

Terrance was floundering and saw soldiers heaving themselves onto broken bits of ships, trying to paddle out towards the ships that couldn't get close enough into them. We had to swim for our lives. By this time, Leslie's face was so swollen that Terrance could hardly see. There were two soldiers who had clambered onto a piece of wreckage, so Terrance swam to them, hoisting himself up onto it, but there wasn't enough room and others were trying to clamber on board. If they managed to clamber on board too, we would have overturned and we'd all be tossed into the sea. Terrance was having nothing of that. So, Terrance, being Terrance, to save himself, kicked out at the faces of the others who, with their last bit of strength, were trying to get on board, seeing them go under in the swirling water. Nasty, but that was Terrance. He didn't care if they drowned, just had to save himself and the body.

Chapter 18

Superintendent R Spooner, was meeting Superintendent T Bowman, head of Leeds C.I.D. They were engaged in the city. Supt Bowman told the Yorkshire Post, "Superintendent Spooner is here on routine inquiries."

They were there trying to get further information from Green's remaining family members, checking statements at the Metropole Hotel and searching places Green had been to try to find the lost jewellery.

The Yorkshire Evening Post, reported on Wednesday, 20 August 1952 that Chief Det-Super T Lockley had advised that the papers in the case were now in the hands of the Director of Public Prosecutions. Within two or three days, it would be possible to consult the Court about a date for the preliminary hearing.

●Moving a section of the kitchen floor which bore vital evidence — a shoeprint
made by the killer.

(Courtesy of the Stoke Sentinel)

On Thursday, September 11, a magistrate and Court officials went to inspect a piece of flooring on which the prosecution alleged was a footmark. I, as the accused, was taken along, handcuffed, escorted by a police officer and. surrounded by police officers. The 2cwt piece of flooring was too heavy to bring into Court and it was decided to adjourn to the yard. One of the police officers identified the piece of flooring as a section of tiled flooring from the home of Mr and Mrs Wiltshaw. What I saw on the floor was the imprint of a shoe. The officer said this imprint had been made when water had poured out of a broken saucepan. Yes, I knew the flooring – I'd walked over it many a time.

We then returned to the Courtroom, which stood on the main road through town, I entered the dock. Leslie was still wearing my green suit, yellow shirt and white spotted maroon tie. My heart was pounding as to what would come out of this inspection. Leslie sat there, almost motionless throughout the Hearing, listening intently to counsel's opening speech and to the witnesses.

Mr Thomas, the prosecutor, said that a pair of bloodstained gloves were found outside the house. There was a button found near the body, the same button missing from one of the gloves as it matched the button still in situ on the other glove.

Mr Thomas went on to say, "Mrs Wilshaw's assailant probably struck the initial blows in the kitchen and then probably went upstairs to get the jewellery. He must have been surprised hearing a noise downstairs and went to investigate. There the assailant found Mrs Wiltshaw somewhere between the kitchen and the hall, and attacked her again. She had many fractures of the skull and lower jaw."

He continued, "At this point there is no direct evidence to show Green had been there and no admission in any statement he has made. Green has denied all along that this was his hand that had caused the injuries.

There is, however, an abundance of circumstantial evidence, which in the submission of the prosecution is of a compelling nature, evidence which quite clearly connects Green with the commission of the crime,"

The first on the stand was Nora, the first of 11 people giving evidence. She confirmed that she was Miss Nora Lammey, a nurse living at Woodhouse Lane, Leeds.

The stand was just two yards from where I was seated. Speaking so softly that, at times, her voice was drowned by the noise of the traffic outside, she told of my visits to Northern Ireland with her.

"I met him in Leeds and we started datin'. I knew he was living in Stoke but he would come to see me in Leeds most weekends. I had holiday booked to see me family in Ireland, so I did, and twice Terry..... I will call him Terry as that's what he said is name was, well twice Terry flew over to visit me there. During one visit, we went to a clergyman and got a marriage certificate. It was after that, back in Leeds that Terry presented me with two rings. I thought it very strange, I mean, why give me the rings now. He should have given me one for our engagement and one to keep for our wedding."

That's when I beckoned to my solicitor, Mr O K Own. I wanted to let him know that I wanted Nora to try the rings on to see that they fitted first.

Nora was continuing, "I later returned the rings to Terry."

Mr Thomas intervened, "So, why did you return the rings?"

"May I sit down before answering that. I feel a bit weak."

A chair was provided for her. She may have been nervous as I was so close to her, so I made sure I looked directly in front and not in her direction.

Nora continued, "My sister, in Ireland, had been visited by the police, asking if she or I knew a Leslie Green, who was wanted for the muerder of Mrs Wiltshaw. My sister told me to be wary. Well, it all seemed a bit strange to me. He'd told me he was rich, but he was always borrowing money from me, then all of a sudden he has the money to buy what looked like very expensive rings. T'ings just didn't add up and I wanted to make sure Terry was who he said he was, and he wasn't mixed up with the robbery and muerder. I wasn't going to accept the rings until they had found the real muerderer. Terry told me he had nothing to do with the murder and said that, if he had done the robbery, it would not have involved muerder. It would have been done in a different way. Well, that got me even more wary. He had told me he was the nephew of Mr Wiltshaw, had a lovely car, had a good job, so why would he think of doing a robbery?"

Leslie was making notes on a pad on his knee during the long Hearing.

The judge adjourned the Court eventually adding, "With the number of witnesses still to be heard, it is not expected that the Hearing will be completed until Monday or Tuesday."

....

When the Hearing was resumed on Monday, one of the witness to be called was Prof. J M Webster, head of the West Midlands Forensic Science Laboratory at Birmingham. He gave an account of the injuries sustained by Mrs Wiltshaw, leading to her death.

"Mrs Wilshaw had been a healthy person for her age. She had a stiff elbow joint, which would render that limb extremely ineffective for both offence and defence. She had three stab wounds in the stomach, the lower jaw and the right shoulder.

The lower and upper jaws were shattered and there was a gross wound across the face, starting on the left of the bridge of the nose and finishing about half an inch from the right ear. There was also a long wound on the left side of the face.

The top of the skull had been beaten in and multiple blows had been struck with a blunt instrument. In my opinion weapons used included a poker and logs of wood. A stabbing instrument not particularly sharp could have caused the wounds to the face and right shoulder. In the case of the stabbing, great force must have been used.

Mrs Wiltshaw's blood was Group A and bloodstains on a number of articles were of the same group and could have been her blood."

Professor Webster continued, "I examined Green's hands on July 30th, and found three notable injuries on the front of his right wrist, in his right palm and on the thumb of his left hand.

The last-named wound corresponded with damage to the left glove of the pair it was stated earlier in the proceedings had been found in the garden of the house. All those wounds could have been caused on or about July 16th."

Mr Thomas posed a question about indications of defence wounds. Replying, Professor Webster said, "The bruising of the ring finger of Mrs Wiltshaw's left hand was caused when she tried to ward off a blow. It was not consistent with the forceful removal of a ring, assuming that there was a ring on the finger."

Professor Webster continued, "It is in my medical opinion that Mrs Wilshaw died from shock and bleeding due to multiple injuries, which included fractures of the skull and fractures of the lower jaw. Death had not been instantaneous."

There was a loud murmur in the room as the crowd heard that, and the Magistrate bring his gavel down on the desk shouting out "Order in Court".

After the murmur died away, the Magistrate indicated, "You may continue Prof Webster."

"When I was handed a bent iron poker with a barb turning outwards at the end, I found human blood of Group A.

Some of the injuries on Mrs Wilshaw's head could have been caused by the poker, but they could also have been made by logs of logs. I examined two logs and found on one of them stains which were of human blood Group A.

The poker could have been responsible for the long wound on the left side of the face and three very terrible wounds on the right side."

There were low murmurings again, but these soon subsided as the Magistrate fixed his beady eyes on the crowd with gavel raised.

Nora was called again. She was smartly dressed in a grey two-piece suit.

She again said that she met me fairly regularly at the weekends and that I once took her by car to a medical ball in Leeds. She again spoke of the holiday to her parents' farm in Ballymena, Moneymore, Northern Ireland where I had visited her twice by plane.

"I accepted his proposal of marriage and we went to visit a clergyman to get a marriage certificate."

Mr Thomas asked, "Did you believe him to be single?"
"Yes."

"You believed that?"
"Yes."

"He had told you so?"

"Yes He gave me to understand that he was wealthy and had travelled to America. On July 10th we returned from Northern Ireland to Leeds and Terry stayed at the Hotel Metropole."

"Was there mention of a lost mackintosh from the Hotel Metropole?"
"Yes, I believe it was July 13th. Terry told me that he had lost his mackintosh and wallet from the cloakroom at the hotel. He said he had reported its loss to the police, but he needed money to tie him over. So I lent him 30s, so I did.

"Had you previously lent him sums of money?"
"Yes. On two separate occasions, £8 and £5.

"So, he was having difficulty paying his bills, having, as he told you, had his wallet stolen. How indeed did he pay for his hotel bill?"

"Terry told me that he was having his bill at the Metropole deferred until he was able to get home to get some more money, then return to Leeds."

"So, Green returned to Stoke-on-Trent, presumably to get money. Did he return?"

"I next saw him on July 17th, when he called for me at the nursing home. We had some drinks together at the Hotel Metropole and, on the way there, that's when he gave me the two rings. They were pure class. I tried them on but one was a bit large."

At this point, Nora was handed two rings, which she identified to be the same rings.

"Did Green say he was giving you the rings for any particular purpose?"

"Not really. He never actually said he was giving them me, though I presumed they were for me and for our engagement and wedding. I t'ink he just wanted me to try them on to see if they fitted.

"Did you show anyone else the rings?"

"Later that night, I showed them to a colleague, I remember Nurse Davis actually asking him how he could afford them, to which Terry replied that the Leeds police had found his wallet."

"Now, Miss Lammey. Due to the nature of this crime, the killer would possibly have had some scratches about his person. Could you say if you noticed any such thing on Green?"

"Well, he did have a bandage on his wrist and Sister Turner, who I work with, said that the police were looking for someone with scratches."

"Quite, Miss Lammey."

That's when Leslie indicated to his solicitor, Mr Own, saying, "They'll find loads of scratches on me!"

"So, Miss Lammey, you mentioned before that you had received a letter from your sister in Belfast."

"Yes, I received the letter on July 18th. I read the letter out to Terry and told him that the police had been to my sister's hame, looking for a man named Leslie Green. I asked him direct if he were the man they were looking for but he told me Green was a common enough name and he said it wasna him He said, though, that he was willing to go to the Garda, I mean the police, and clear up any possible link to him and the muerderer."

………………

It was day three of the Hearing:

"You've got quite a fan club here Green," my guard said, as I waiting in the cell to go up the steps to the little courtroom, "Yes, there's been a queue of people waiting more than an hour today, outside the public entrance to the Court – loads of women too."

The two Scotland Yard detectives, Detective-Superintendent Reginald W Spooner and Detective-Sergeant Ernest Millen, gave evidence today, reporting on the police station interviews.

Mr Geoffrey Lionel Farr, manager of the Station Hotel, Stafford was called to the stand. "I saw Green in the bar at the hotel at about 12.30pm on July 16. Green went into lunch with two other men and they finished their meal about 3.30pm. The next time I saw Green was about 6.30pm or 6.35pm in the evening.

Green told me that he had been across to the station, had fallen asleep and had missed his train. He was carrying a holdall and an RAF-type mackintosh was on top of it. Green asked for a wash and also inquired the times of the trains to Leeds."

"So quite significant, Mr Farr, that Green was carrying an RAF-type mackintosh."

The defending counsel objected to this, stating that it could possibly have been another mackintosh, not necessarily Mr Wiltshaw's.

Next on the stand was a waitress at the hotel, Mrs Maria Caroline Coulman, of Beech Avenue, Stafford. She said, "Green and the two other men had wine for lunch, and then one suggested I should take the bill to another man sitting in the dining room. I next saw Green in the evening about 7pm, when he had dinner. He was in the dining room about 15 or 20 minutes."

"Did you know the two other men, Mrs Coulman?"

"Sorry, no. I had not seen them before and there were not registered at the hotel."

"Could you perhaps describe them, Mrs Coulman?"
"I'm sorry sir, there are so many people coming through the hotel, although, from what I remember, and I'm not certain about this, was that one was older, in his early 40s I would say, well-built with

124

dark hair, clean-shaven. The other was a bit younger – clean-shaven too, but thinner than the first man, with a thin face."

"Thank you Mrs Coulman. You may stand down."

....

After the last of the 45 witnesses had been heard, Mr Ryland Thomas (for the Director of Public Prosecutions) asked me, "Do you at this stage wish to call witnesses or to give evidence?"

"I am not guilty." I called out.

"That is what the forthcoming trial will prove, one way or the other, Mr Green."

"So, I repeat, do you wish to call witnesses or to give evidence at the present time?"

".... I am not guilty and I reserve my defence." I replied.

Mr Ryland Thomas (for the Director of Public Prosecutions) then formally asked the Magistrate (Mr E F Goodhill) to commit me to trial at Stafford if he found that a *prima facie* case had been made out.

Mr E F Goodill (Magistrate) then spoke to the courtroom, looking at me. "Leslie Green, you have identified yourself as being 29 years of age, a native of Leeds and an unemployed motor driver. I am committing you to Stafford Assizes to be tried on a charge of murdering Mrs Alice Maud Mary Wiltshaw, of Estoril, Barlaston, near here, wife of a pottery manufacturer.

He then turned to face the Court. "The Assizes at Stafford will open on November 27 and the Judges will be either Mr Justice Stable or Mr Justice Pritchard."

My defence council approached the bench and I could just make out that he was asking, because of the great publicity in this case, that the case should be heard at an assize in another country.

The Magistrate rejected this application.

About an hour after the proceedings had ended I was driven out of the police station yard in a police van on the way to Shrewsbury Prison.

I could hear crowds lining the pavements, outside the little Courtroom. I suppose they were there in the hope of catching a glimpse of me as I was taken away. Some were shouting out obscenities. "Hang the bastard" and such like. I smiled to myself. Notoriety is a bit like fame, Terry thought – so fame at last – I was famous!

Chapter 19
Day 1, Monday, December 1st 1952

The trial began on Monday, December 1st, 1952. The jury had been sworn in.

I was represented by Mr G G Baker and Mr G T Meredith.
Mr E Ryder Richardson, QC appeared for the Crown with Mr J F Bourke. The judge was Mr Justice Stabple.

Mr Richardson's opening statement occupied 80 minutes. In his opening speech he told the jury:

"Mrs Wiltshaw was killed at about 6pm on the evening of July 16th. She was very fond of jewellery and used to wear a lot. There was always jewellery in the house, kept in the top drawer of the dressing table in the first floor bedroom, which she shared with her husband. There was about £3,000 worth of jewellery left in the house in the drawer.

The rear of the house was never locked. That was the position on the night of July 16th.

When her husband returned that night, he came back a little earlier than usual, about 6.20pm. He walked in by the back door, which was open. In the kitchen there was what he described as chaos.

I will describe the scene that Mr Wiltshaw walked into. Saucepans, potatoes and Mrs Wiltshaw's spectacles were found on the floor. There was blood on a table cloth and on the walls.

Mr Wiltshaw thought there had been a terrible accident

He rushed to the hall and met as terrible a sight as could ever meet a husband's eyes, for his wife was lying dead, terribly battered about the head. Beside her lay an old-fashioned poker.

She was practically unrecognisable. Mrs Wiltshaw had apparently put up a most determined resistance. The attack had started in the kitchen and she had gone from there to the hall where the murdered had finished her off in a most dreadful manner."

The poker was undoubtedly the weapon which had caused her many grievous injuries. There was also lying beside her a shattered vase, another weapon which probably caused some of her injuries. Mrs Wiltshaw was practically unrecognisable. She had seven stab wounds in the body.

Her assailant had finished her off in the most ghastly manner in the hall.

A doctor was called and later the doctor and Mr Wiltshaw walked out into the garden, probably for a breath of fresh air, and the husband there saw on the garden path, leading to a wicket gate, a gate that was not known to many people, a pair of wash-leather gloves, bloody, with a cut on the top of the thumb of the left glove.

It looked as though the murderer, running away, had taken off the gloves he was wearing and thrown them down on the path.

Returning to his wife's body, Mr Wiltshaw noticed that there were no rings on his wife's hands. It struck him that it was strange because she usually wore the rings. There was no sign of a search for jewellery as far as could be seen and it seemed as if her assailant had done his ghastly deed and gone away.

The next startling discovery was that the whole of the valuable jewellery valued at about £3,000 had gone. Among it were two valuable diamond rings, one an eternity ring, the other a baguette ring, a gold bracelet on which were original charms and a gold cigarette case.

Later it was found that an RAF-type mackintosh was missing. It was easily identifiable because the belt had got into a twisted shape by careless use and there was a burn mark made by a cigarette on the left side of the coat in front.

It was obvious that the murderer had known a good deal about the pattern of life at Estoril. He had known the hour at which to attack, and he might probably have made friends with the dog, as the dog was known to bark at strangers. It looked as though he had known where the jewellery had been kept and, as if he knew the back way out of the house.

The police began to suspect every person who knew these facts and every person who could fit into them. It came to their knowledge that Green had worked as chauffeur-handyman for the Wiltshaws for nearly two years, and the police wanted to see him to ask about his movements. On Wednesday, July 23, one week after the murder, Green went voluntarily to Longton (Staffordshire) Police Station."

Richardson then went on to say, "Green had made a long statement in which, he alleges that after his dismissal by Mr Wiltshaw, he obtained other work but became unemployed on July 1st. He spoke of his association with Nurse Nora Lammey, of the Clarement Nursing Home, Clarendon Road, Leeds, and said that he had been to Leeds as often as he could to see her.

Green also alleges that he spoke of travelling to Stafford, where he said he intended to see his wife to make a fresh start, but that,

129

when he got to Stafford, he could not make up his mind what to do and did not see his wife. Later he said that, on the day of the murder, he was no nearer Barlaston than Stafford."

....

Leslie's mind returned to that day. Yes, I'd been on the train, then walking around, trying to make up my mind what I should say to Constance. Yes, I was also pondering on trying to make it up with her, make a fresh start. I didn't really know what I'd been doing all this time in Leeds, just remember bits and pieces. I knew I had a girlfriend, so I'd been playing away, but so much was lost to me, which I had no memory of. It was as though I'd been walking around in a dream. I needed to see a doctor but I was scared what they'd say. I had tickets in my pockets, train tickets to London and Birmingham and even one to Torquay. What had I been doing in Torquay, for heaven's sake? Maybe I was looking for work in all of these places, who knows? I thumped my palm against my head, over and over, but that didn't help, just gave me a bit of a headache. I couldn't remember if I actually went to see Constance, whether I spoke to her. I remember going there, that's all.

What happened was that I took over, Terry that is. Yes, Leslie did go to see Constance but he never went in to speak to her. Instead he hid in an outhouse and fell asleep there, not daring to go in. It was the early hours after all. I couldn't wake Constance, but with all my banging and shouting, Constance appeared. She had been staying next door. She let me in. Yes, there was a bit of a row, to say the least, when I told her about Nora Lammey. So I put an end to Leslie pondering on whether to get back with his wife. Constance said she had an inkling that there was someone else on the scene. She sent me packing and I went back to Stafford. Of course, Lesley had no idea he had seen her and, poor thing,

130

was still pondering about seeing her as he wandered around Stafford before going to the Stafford Hotel.

………………..

Again referring to my statement, Mr Richardson continued, "Green alleged that he spoke of staying at the Hotel Metropole in Leeds, where he used the name of Wiltshaw, and he later gave a detailed account of how the rings had come into his possession."

Mr Richardson went on, "Green started getting into low water financially. He was borrowing money from Miss Lammey, to whom he was pretending to be a well-to-do young man and a traveller connected with the pottery business. While he was representing himself to be well-off, he went to a man and asked to borrow money. That was after his first flying visit to Ireland.

The second time Green went to Ireland, he returned with Miss Lammey to Leeds and booked in at the Hotel Metropole. He stayed there on July 11th, 12th, and 13th. By July 13th, about three days before the murder, he was in desperate straits for money. He went back again to the man from whom he had tried unsuccessfully to borrow and said he wanted about £20 at least.

Green told him that he had the hotel bill to pay. He could not borrow any money from this man, but he managed to persuade the staff manager at the Hotel Metropole to allow his bill to stand over on the assurance that he would come back later and pay it.

In the early morning of July 14th, Green left Leeds for London and stayed at the Strand Palace Hotel. While he was there, he wrote, in the name of Wiltshaw, asking for accommodation to be reserved for him at the Hotel Metropole on July 17th.

131

Green arrived at Stafford on July 16th and went to the Station Hotel. He had lunch, which he finished about 3.30pm, and so far as the prosecution could ascertain, he was next in the hotel about 6.30 or 6.35pm.

....

Yes, I (Leslie) remember going to Stafford and having dinner there, and I had quite a few pints afterwards. I know I was going to go back to Leeds and made my way to the station, but I came over really tired, probably from so much booze, sat down on a bench and fell asleep. When I woke I felt hungry again so thought I'd go back to the Stafford hotel for a bite to eat, then make my way to Leeds from there.

....

The manager saw him about 3.30pm and the next time he saw him was when he came up the steps of the hotel at about 6.35, carrying a bag."

Mr Richardson went on: "If the prosecution is right, you will probably think he had plenty of time to go 10 miles or so to commit murder and come back. He would not want to get there before 5.30pm and he would want to have left as soon as his objective was achieved.

The hotel manager noticed that on the top of his bag was an R.A.F.-type raincoat. Green had an evening meal there, left the hotel caught a train to Leeds, arriving at the Hotel Metropole about 12.30am. Green paid his hotel bill.

Green then went to the nursing home, where Miss Lammey worked, and there he showed two beautiful rings to Nurse Turner, who worked with her."

Mr Richardson then emphasised, "I submit that these rings were Mrs Wiltshaw's rings, undoubtedly stolen at the time the murder was committed.

The next day Green visited Miss Lammey and gave her two rings. He was introduced to Nurse Davies, who worked at the same nursing home and who lived with her husband in a flat in Belmont Road, Leeds.

Mr Richardson concluded his opening speech saying, "Miss Lammey had gone to Ireland on her annual holidays towards the end of June and twice Green had flown over to see her and, during one of these visits, they had become engaged."

Nora Lammey was called again. The Judge asked, "At that time on 17th July, had you read about the death of Mrs Wiltshaw in the papers?"

"Only a short account," was her reply.

Judge: "Up to that time, had it crossed your mind in any shape or form Green could possibly be connected with the murder?"

"No, sir."

She went into great detail about her connections with me, continuing to our meeting in the Park Square Garden, in Leeds.

"Well, we went for a walk in Park Square Garden. It had been a grand aul day, I mean it had been sunny and was still warem, so it was – then we went into another park in Clarendon Road. Terry never said a word about the moehrder, except to say that he

133

dedn't do it, but I do remember him mentioning his friend, Charlie. He said he t'ought he knew who had killed Mrs Wiltshaw.".

The Judge then intervened, "Would you mind telling us in – if I may say so – the vulgar tongue, if you wish, what he did say?"

"He said that at one time Charles had asked him about house-breaking."

"Did that ruffle your composure, Miss Lammey?"
"No."

"What mental process, if any, did you pass through when the name Charles was mentioned? What did you think we was talking about?"

"I t'ought it was someone he knew. Terry also said the police wanted to see him because he had been employed as a chauffeur with the Wiltshaws."

"Was that the first occasion that Green made any mention about the Wilshaw family?"

"Yes."

"Was that the very first occasion it had ever crossed your mind that he had anything to do with the Wiltshaw family?"

"Yes."

Geoffrey Lionel Farr, manager of Station Hotel, Stafford was next on the stand. He spoke about me arriving at the hotel for lunch, saying I was drinking with four other people and had stayed in the bar for two hours, then going to the dining room with two other men, leaving at about 3.30pm.

134

He went on to say, "The next time I saw Green was about 6.30pm, when Green came back into the hotel. I asked him what he was doing back, as I understood from the conversation during lunchtime that he was going to catch a train. Green told me he had gone across to the station but had fallen asleep on the platform.

He had an RAF-type grip and an RAF-type raincoat with him. He asked for a wash and a meal. He then looked at a timetable and said he wanted to go to Leeds. I said to him that, as he was having a meal, he would not have time to catch the 7.07 train to Leeds, but there was one leaving at about 7.50 that evening."

Mr Wiltshaw was called to the stand. He added to his statement that he found his wife's poodle dog outside the house, when he returned home on the day of the murder. It was looking very distressed and whimpering, The back gate had been left open, which was unusual. He had no doubt that the RAF-type mackintosh, produced in Court, was his property.

Superintendent Lockley was next up. Replying to further questions he agreed that one woman picked out a man, whose movements were later checked by the police. It was found that he could not possibly have been in the district that day."

Asked about the gloves, Lockley stated, "I had asked the accused to try the gloves on and noticed that the small hole on the pad of the thumb of the left-hand glove matched exactly with a small abrasion on Green's thumb."

I spoke to Mr Own, "They've made that 'ole to match the cut on me thumb." I suppose I was just trying to grab at anything to help my case. Mr Own basically replied that he could not put that

135

statement forward, it would not be accepted, plus the hole in the glove was noted well before I presented myself at Longton Police Station.

Lockley was also asked about the footprints in the kitchen by my defence, "Now, there must have been numerous people paddling about on that kitchen floor, walking over evidence, don't you agree?"

Lockley replied, "To be exact, six police officers, six civilians and myself."

"Point made" defence replied.

After further questioning Lockley stated, "Green had given fairly accurate descriptions of men he had seen in the Station Hotel. On the afternoon of the murder no-one had complained to the police that a car had been missed from the Station Hotel. Anyone travelling by bus from Stafford to Barlaston by the main road would have a walk of a mile from the bus stop to the Wiltshaws' house. It was, however, only three minutes' quick walk or run from the railway station to the house.

Other witnesses stated that he had been known at the Metropole Hotel as Mr Wiltshaw.

The prosecution alleged that I had murdered Mrs Wiltshaw, stole some of the jewellery and had managed to get back to Leeds within a few hours.

My defence queried whether that was at all possible and various time tables were brought into Court to check over and ratify.

The ticket collector at Stafford Station gave evidence: " I spoke to Green at 7.20pm, for about 10 or 15 minutes. This was after the 7.07pm train had left. The next train was due at 7.50pm."

Mrs Greta Davies, a nurse at the Claremont Nursing Home, Leeds gave evidence that she had seen me at the nursing home, but only for about five minutes, but that she did see me again on July 17th, when Miss Lammey accompanied me to her own flat at about 10.20pm. Miss Lammey had taken Green round to introduce him to her husband. "I noticed that he had two rings on his little finger."

She continued, "I invited Miss Lammey and Green to tea at my flat the next day, Friday, July 18th. We got talking and were getting on nicely. My husband and I could see that he liked Nora – Miss Lammey – and we offered Green our flat for the weekend, as we usually went away at weekends. He was very happy as he didn't have anywhere to stay except the hotel.

When we got back we all got talking and Terry – I mean Green - said his aunt had been brutally attacked with an old-fashioned poker. He said that it had been a very brutal murder. He then added his aunt was Mrs Wiltshaw. Green told me he had hired a car and been down to Stone, Staffordshire to see his uncle. His uncle had told him to get on his way back as they were roping everyone in."

"Thank you for that Mrs Davies", Richardson replied, "However, I understand Leeds police have since visited your flat. Do you know what they were looking for?"

"Yes, sir, I was there when a police officer found the two rings. The same ones Green had been wearing on his little finger. The officer actually found them in the coal cellar at the flat – lodged behind a brick."

"Thank you Mrs Davies."

The next up was a Mr Alfred Blackburn, of Prosperity Street, Leeds, "I was patient in the Claremont Nursing Home from June 15th – I was there for three weeks. I met Green while I was there. He was asking for money for petrol. Then I saw 'im again on Sunday, July 13th. He actually came to my 'ome, wouldst tha believe it, asking again to borrow some money. This time he wanted to pay a bill of about £10 that he owed the Hotel Metropole. I told him to get lost on both occasions.

I 'appened to see 'im again a couple of days later, I believe it was the 17th – actually in the Metropole. This time he pulled out a wallet, showing me several one pound notes. He was quite sarcastic and smarmy like, asking me if I wanted to borrow owt."

Gwenith D Jenkins, a receptionist at the Metropole, Leeds was next up. She said, "Green had been to the hotel on a number of occasions. I knew him as Mr Wiltshaw, of Estoril, Barlaston". He signed in on July 16th, under the name of Wiltshaw, giving his address as Barlaston. He had been to the hotel earlier that month."

Mr Ryder Richardson, QC, for the prosecution, then asked if the hotel had received any written communication from Green.

Miss Jenkins replied, "Yes, but as I said, under the name of Wiltshaw. The hotel received a letter headed, 'Wiltshaw Strand Palace Hotel, Stand, London'. He wanted a room reserved for him on 17th July. It was signed 'Terry Wiltshaw'. I saw him on the morning of July 17th when he asked me for his outstanding account, which he then paid off.

I saw him a little while later as he came I back to the reception office with a newspaper in his hand. This would be about 10

138

minutes after I had first seen him. He said he had read that his aunt had been murdered and he would have to go back home. He did not say where his home was, but I knew it as 'Estoril'. He left later that morning, but before leaving asked for his room to be kept, and said he might be back that night."

R Kenneth Dean, a porter at the Metropole, told of Green's arrival at the hotel about 12.30am on the night of July 16th-17th.

"He asked for a room, saying he had already reserved a room for the following night, but had come to Leeds unexpectedly. He then offered me a cigarette from a case, which appeared to be gold. I'd never seen him with a cigarette case before."

Kenneth Beasley, night porter at the Metropole, said, "I got talking with Green. I suppose that would be about 11pm on July 17th. Green 'appened to mention the murder so I naturally asked if Mrs Wiltshaw was a relation. Green said that if it was his aunt and that he had been to Stafford to see if there was anything he could do. There wasn't, so he'd come back."

Mr Beasley continued, "I said to him that it was a nasty business. Green replied, "I don't know why anyone who would want to do her any harm, because she never did any harm to anybody."

I told Green I'd read in the papers that nothing was missing and Green replied that that was unbelievable as there were plenty of antiques and silver in the home."

George Alleroyde, formerly a porter at the Metropole, said he knew Green as Mr Wiltshaw. He added, "On the morning of July 17th, Green asked me for some lint, saying he had a sore on his wrist. I didn't ask him how he got the injury, but Green said of his own volition 'That is what you get by opening windows to let the girl friend in'."

139

Cross-examined by Mr G G Baker for the defence, Mr Alleroyde said he understood Green damaged his wrist at the Claremont Nursing Home.

Mr H W King, staff manager of the Metropole, said that on July 13th Green asked him to defer the payment of his hotel bill, as he had lost his raincoat and wallet.

Green promised that he would pay his bill when he returned to the hotel.

A receptionist at the hotel, Miss Pauline Fenton, said that she saw Green and sympathised with him on the death of his aunt. "He told me that he had been down to the house, but it was full of police. He added that he knew that she (his aunt) had been a bad old thing, but he was sorry that she had gone."

Policewoman Edna M Bowers said that she was at Longton police station, near Stafford, on July 23 when, at about 9.15am, Green walked in and said: "I am the man you are all shouting about."

Policewoman Bowers said that she asked him his name and Green replied: "I am the Leslie Green."

Prof James M Webster, director of the Home Office Laboratory, Birmingham, said he made a post-mortem examination on Mrs Wiltshaw's body.

He found she had stab wounds in the stomach, shoulder and neck, which could have been caused by the point of an ornamental poker, found near the body; gashes on the face, which could have been caused by blows from the poker, and from injury to the top of the head and jaw, which could have been caused by blows from logs thrown at her.

The Judge told him that it would not be necessary for him to go into minute detail of the wounds to Mrs Wiltshaw's body. Speaking to the Court he stated, "I have also withheld several photographs from the jury as being too distressing for them to see."

After Prof. Webster had detailed other injuries, he agreed with the Judge that it was a human machine battered out of all recognition.

He said, "I have taken a sample of Green's blood, which is Group O. On the inside sleeve of an RAF-type mackintosh, he found blood stains of Group O. I examined Green's clothes for bloodstains, but did not find any."

When I examined Green I found two scrape abrasions on the right hand and forearm and a small healed superficial wound on the left thumb."

Cross-examined: Prof Webster, the defendant has advised me that he received the cut to his wrist from a fall onto stone steps while he was out walking. With your medical knowledge, could you rule out these abrasions being caused by a fall?"

Prof Webster was not able to counter that and advised that the abrasions could indeed have been caused by a fall.

There was a surprise later in the afternoon when the prosecution called a nurse from the Claremont Nursing Home, Leeds, someone who had not previously appeared in the proceedings.

She was Nurse Sylvia Fitchley, and she said that she was on duty at the home on the night of July 16th -17th, when Green went to see Miss Lammey.

"I let Green in about 12.45am. He went to the nurses' sitting room and asked if he could see Nurse Lammey, Nurse Lammey said 'No'.

I sat down with him and Sister Turner in the sitting-room, where we had some coffee and sandwiches. That's when Green showed me two rings. I thought, that's nice, he's got them for Nurse Lammey. I then started doing a crossword puzzle." To which Mr Justice Stable stated, "You seem to suffer from the same complaint as I do, which crossword puzzle was it? (This prompted laughter in the Court)

Taking the stand, Supt R W Spooner of Scotland Yard, said that on July 23 he saw Green at Longton police station.

Super Spooner said, "I saw Green again on July 24th. This time Supt Lockley of Staffordshire CID) told me that Green (with a nod in my direction) had said he didn't do the murder, but he knows he is involved in it and perhaps responsible."

Harry Grimley, from the railway police was brought to the stand. He stated that he had found a ticket, bought at Barlaston, bought on 16th July and handed in at Leeds. This was the same train that the mackintosh was found on.

This caused a murmur in the audience and jury.

Richardson, addressing the jury: "So, from Mr Grimley report, it looks like our culprit took that train on his way to meet his girlfriend in Leeds."

My defending counsel then spoke to the Jury saying, "My learned friend will try to turn your attention to what he says will be facts that the defendant was the only person who could have committed

142

the atrocious murder. What I put to you, members of the jury, is that all that you will hear will be circumstantial evidence – nothing concrete to prove that the defendant was ever at the property on the day in question and I wish you to bear that in mind during the Court proceedings.

My learned friend has also stated that the ticket bought at Barlaston, bought on 16th July and handed in at Leeds, was the same train that the mackintosh was found on. Again, I urge you all to acknowledge that this could just be circumstantial evidence. Anyone else could have bought a ticket at Barlaston, going through to Leeds."

After the numerous statements had been heard, the Judge announced that he believed the trial would not finish until the end of the week. It was expected that he would start his summing-up on Thursday afternoon. The trial would continue tomorrow.

Chapter 20

Day 2, Tuesday, December 2 1952

It was my 30th birthday and here I was again, in the dock, facing a murder trial.

The prosecution's first witness today was Scotland Yard's fingerprint expert, det. Chief-Inspector Edwin Holten. He said that he had examined a pair of shoes found in the hold-all belonging to Green and also the tiled kitchen floor of Estoril's kitchen.

He himself had worn one of the shoes, which had been inked to get a footprint. In his opinion a footprint found on the grey tiled kitchen floor could have been made by one of the shoes.

There was an objection from my counsel, "My Lord, Chief-Inspector Holten is not saying for definite that the shoes could have made the same imprint. May I add candidly and I wish it to be noted, that he used the word 'could'- the imprint could have been made by one of the shoes."

"Duly noted, counsel for the defence."

My counsel suggested to the Judge, Mr Justice Stable, that the jury should see the original piece of flooring cut from the kitchen at 'Estoril'. Mr Justice Stable duly acknowledged this and adjourned the trail for 10 minutes allowing time for himself and the 12 members of the jury to examine the piece of concrete flooring. The Judge agreed that he and the jury should see both the photographs and the original exhibit, rather than that they should see only photographs. The flooring weighed about three cwt and could not be brought into the courtroom. It had been placed in a room at the Assize Court building. This was the same piece of flooring I had viewed during the Hearing, on which there was a footprint.

During the late afternoon, the jury were asked to leave the Court while the Judge heard legal argument about the admissibility of certain statements. When they returned, the Judge told them that he had decided that the statements were admissible. All day I sat in the dock with my arms folded, just speaking once, in a whispered discussion with my counsel, Mr G G Baker, Q C, who was seated with Mr G T Meredith, just to ask how he thought the trial was going.

Mr Richardson's opening statement occupied 80 minutes.

'When Miss Lammey, who was smartly dress in a black feathered hat and a red-and-black checked coat, went into the witness box, Mr Justice Stable said he realised it was a distressing occasion for her and gave her permission to sit down while giving her evidence.

"So, can you tell the Court the course of events after meeting Green, Miss Lammey?"

She said, "When I first met Green in April, he said his name was Terry Green. After the first meeting we met almost every weekend and on May 2, when he visited Leeds in a Rover car, he took me to a dance.

Mr Justice Stable: "Were you friends or more than friends?"
Miss Lammey: "We were more than friends and Green had proposed marriage to me in Ireland and I had accepted his proposal."

Miss Lammey said, "Terry did not give me an engagement ring, but said he would get one. I understood that he was quite wealthy."

145

Mr Justice Stable: "Was that a general impression you got, or was it anything he said about his financial position?"

Miss Lammey: "It was a sort of general impression. Terry had told me he was a traveller and had something to do with pottery. He told me he had once travelled to America."

Mr Justice Stable: "And did you know that Green was already married?"

Miss Lammey: "No, sir. It has all come as a great shock to me." at this Nora wiped a tear from her eye and blew her nose. "Sorry sir, but I'm just overcome. You see, we both went to get a marriage certificate when we were in Ireland. To get the certificate we had to take an oat' and give various particulars. Terry said he was single and he gave his Christian names as Terrance and Leslie. That's the first time I'd known that he had a middle name. The certificate meant we could get married at any time."

Miss Lammey said she understood Green lived in Stafford.

She was then shown photographs of Nurse Davies's flat, Miss Lammey said she had never hidden jewellery in the coal place or anywhere else.

Miss Lammey said that about 8.45pm Green met her outside the Claremont Nursing Home, on 16th July. She was surprised as she thought he was getting the 6pm train.

She then told the crowded Assize Court that I had stated that the dead woman was my aunt.

"Terry told me that his aunt had been attacked with an old-fashioned poker and to have called it a 'very brutal murder."

Chapter 21

Day 3, Wednesday, December 3, 1952

Nora Lammey was in the witness box for nearly four hours.

Speaking so softly that, at times, even the Judge, Mrs Justice Stable, who was sitting only three yards away, could not hear her, Miss Lammey told how she and Green had become engaged, visited a Presbyterian clergyman in Ireland to obtain a marriage certificate, and had fixed a date in August, the 9th, "very provisionally" as their wedding day.

Twice the Judge asked her to speak up and once he said: "I realise it is distressing for you, but you must keep your voice up."

When the luncheon interval came, Miss Lammey was still in the witness-box and the Judge ordered that she should have her lunch in a private room, in the Assize building.

After lunch, the prosecuting counsel, Mr Ryder Richardson, Q.C., showed Miss Lammey two valuable rings, which it is alleged had been given to her by Green, and, it is further alleged, had been stolen from Mrs Wiltshaw's house. Miss Lammey was holding the rings in her hand when Mr Richardson told her to take off her glove from her left hand and try the rings on. She did so, but then could not get one of the rings off again.

After Miss Lammey had struggled for a time in the witness-box, the Judge told her to go outside and try to get the ring off. She went out, accompanied by a woman police officer and the proceedings were held up until she returned a few minutes later, holding the ring in her hand.

At the end of her evidence, the Judge suggested a short rest and a cup of tea before counsel for the defence, Mr G G Baker, QC, started his cross-examination. The Judge told her: "I appreciate it is quite an emotional and mental strain. Miss Lammey then left the Court and went to a private room. The Court was adjourned for about 10 minutes.

Miss Lammey, in evidence, spoke of her first meeting with Green (Leslie/Terry) in April this year and my journeys to Leeds to see her, mostly at weekends. "In Leeds he stayed at the Hotel Metropole. She said that she went on holiday to her home in Ireland towards the end of June and twice I flew over to visit her. We became engaged and went to a Presbyterian clergyman where," she said, "we had to give our names, ages and occupations.

On oath, Terry said he was single and gave his Christian names as Terrance and Leslie. She added that, once they had got the certificate, they could have got married at any time. They had discussed marriage and August 9th had been mentioned very provisionally as their wedding day. "I told Terry I proposed to leave my job at the Claremont Nursing Home, Clarendon Road, Leeds, on July 21st, but we had not decided where we were going to live.

On July 9, we came back to England by air. "I went to the nursing home and Terry stayed at the Hotel Metropole." She recalled that, before her holiday, Terry had borrowed £13 from her, but had repaid 30s."

Miss Lammey continued, "Terry stayed in Leeds on July 11th, 12th and 13th, and on the 13th, a Sunday, he told me that his raincoat had been stolen from the Hotel Metropole and that his wallet, containing money, was in one of the pockets."

At this point, Miss Lammey was shown a torn raincoat, but she said she did not recognise it as Green's. Green had a belted mackintosh and the one she had been show, she pointed out, was without a belt.

Mr Richardson then asked her to look at the raincoat As she was examining it, the Judge left his seat, walked along the Bench to the witness-box, picked up the coat and spread it out in front of Miss Lammey. After she had looked at it, the Judge handed it to the jury and remarked that the belt had been removed from it.

Continuing, Miss Lammey said that I had told her I had reported the loss of my raincoat to the police.

She was then questioned about a visit I paid to Leeds, after the murder of Mrs Wilshaw on July 16th. In reply to the Judge, she said, "I had read a short account of the muerder in a newspaper, but it had not crossed my mind that Terry could be connected with it." She went on to tell of my being given permission to stay three nights at the flat in Belmont Grove, Leeds, occupied by a colleague, Nurse Davies, and her husband. On one of the days I met her outside the nursing home.

That day she had had a letter from her sister in Belfast, telling her that the police had been to her house looking for a man named Leslie Green.

Miss Lammey said she told me about what was in the letter. "Terry said he did not know why the police should be looking for him, but he was perfectly willing to go and find out." She added, "At that time I did not know that Terry had had any connection with the Wiltshaw family." (Earlier in the proceedings it was stated that Green was chauffeur-handyman for the Wiltshaws for nearly two years.)

Recalling that Green had previously given her two rings, Miss Lammey said that I later handed her two cases for them, but I'd returned the rings after receiving the letter from my sister.

Judge Stable then snapped at her, seemingly having lost patience with her, "Miss Lammey, try and get some realism into the story."

Physically shaken Nora replied, "I'm sorry sir. I missed out that I had given the rings back after receiving the letter from my sister in Ireland."

On further questioning, she continued: "We both went to see my friend, Mrs Davis, and her husband. They live in a flat in Belmont Grove, in Leeds. They were going away and Mr and Mrs Davis agreed to Terry using their flat for two nights. One of the nights Terry took me to see a play at the Theatre Royal, Leeds – 'It won't be a stylish marriage' - . It were awful good, so it were, if not a little disquieting to me personally as, as you know, I'd retorned the rings to Terry and I started to wonder whether or not our marriage would ever take place, whether it be stylish or not."

Miss Lammey was then questioned about the conversation she had with me in Leeds on the Sunday before I left the city to go to Torquay. She said, "Terry was going to catch the 10.20pm train. We went to the City Station, but found there was not a train until about 11.20pm, so we went, to kill time, to a park in Park Square and sat down on a seat together. When that park was closing we then went to some more gardens in Clarendon Road. It was then that Terry told me for the first time that he was not who I thought he was and that he was out of work. He said he had actually been employed as a chauffeur to the Wiltshaws but insisted he had nothing to do with the muerder."

"So, what happened when this young man you had regarded as pretty well-to-do, in good employment, with his motor-car and able to afford to put up at reasonably expensive hotels and had given you two beautiful rings, and with whom you were anticipating marriage, told you he was not the person he made himself out to be, but out of work?"

"Nothing."

This prompted another outburst from Mr Justice Stable. "Miss Lammey, I find it incredulous that you have shown little or no reaction to this surprising news, seeing that you had just given up your job."

"I am trying to keep calm sir. Yes, I was shocked to the extreme but you must understand, I was still very much in love with Terry and you can't just turn love on and off like that, I can't anyway. We had plans and everything was up in the air now. Terry had lied to me and I had believed every little lie."

The questioning continued: "What mental process, if any, did you go through when the name Charles was mentioned? What did you think he was talking about?"

"I just thought it was someone he knew."

Miss Lammey added, "Terry went on to say that he had backed out of an agreement with 'Charles' to break into the Wiltshaw house."

Nora was now becoming tearful, getting her handkerchief from her bag.

When she had regained her composure, she was questioned further about what I had said my movements were on the day of the murder. "He said he had been in Stafford on that day and had spent the afternoon drinking."

151

On further questioning, Nora said that I took her back to the nursing home and that we had to get in through the sitting room window because the night nurse was deaf and would not hear the bell.

Explaining about Green's journey to Torquay, she said, "Terry told her that he had some business to attend to there, and he thought it would be better if he went there first rather than to Stoke, where he was to have gone originally. I did not ask him what the business was nor did he tell me." That was all that was said about this journey to Torquay.

Continuing her evidence, Miss Lammey said, "I had shown Terry a newspaper on 22nd as his name was mentioned. Terry told me that, if he had done the robbery at the Wiltshaw house, he would have done it a different way."

The judge interjected, "In other words he was saying that, if he had done the murder, it would have not have involved murder."

Miss Lammey agreed.

Cross-examined, Miss Lammey said that I told her I had a Rover car. She said she was suspicious that the rings she had been given had been come by in some wrong manner, so she gave them back to me.

"Terry told me quite a lot about himself when we were in Park Square Gardens. He said he had worked for Mr Wiltshaw, He was not the person he had made himself out to be, and that he had stolen in the past. I t'ink I called him an eejit for lying to me but added that I had an inkling that something was amiss. He said he was really sorry. He also went on to say that he had nothing to do with the murder of Mrs Wiltshaw. He did not mention anybody other than 'Charles'."

I remember that incident. It had been the one time I couldn't really control Leslie. He took over. He must have been desperate to get the truth out.   I was really annoyed with him.   He told her everything about not being who he said he was, being jobless, being a small-time crook. Why did he say that? He'd brought the downfall of the world I had created. He actually also said he felt he was not fit to associate with her.   All I can think of was that he had actually fallen in love with her and didn't want to start their life together with a load of lies. He not only risked losing the world we had built up together, but he risked losing Nora. I couldn't see Nora wanting to associate herself with a low time crook. I suppose, at the back of his mind, he knew he couldn't ever get that bungalow he had promised her and could never live up to her expectations. Funnily enough, though, she must have loved him because she didn't run away in disgust. Maybe she'd had a hunch about what he was and had accepted it. Love, it's got a strong hold! But, from that moment on, I didn't have the same amount of control over Leslie and he would be there, listening in to me whenever I came to the fore. Silly little runt, he would be our demise!

Sister Beatrice Turner, who was formerly employed at the nursing home when Miss Lammey was there, said in evidence that Green told her about the loss of his raincoat, his wallet and a cheque book. On the night of July 16th -17th, Green came to the nursing home about 1 in the morning and asked for something to eat. Green showed her two rings and said that, since he last saw her, they had become engaged.

"I put out my hand to take the ring off his finger," Sister Turner said, "but he said he must not take them off as he might lose them." Green then told her that the rings were for Miss Lammey.

He offered her a cigarette from a gold case which, she said, was smaller than the usual type of case, and was round at the corners.

When she asked to look at the cigarette case, Green did not say anything, but just closed it and put it away. Previously he had offered her cigarettes from boxes or from packets. She had never seen him with a cigarette case before. She asked him how he had travelled to Leeds and he said that he had got a lift in a car and that he had just arrived. Later she saw Green with a wallet and cheque book, which he said the police had returned to him.

Sister Turner recalled that she noticed a bandage on Green's left wrist and she told him jokingly that he had better be careful because the police were looking for a man with scratches. Earlier he had told her that his aunt had been murdered and he had been down to see about it. It was because he said that, that she remarked about the scratches.

After Sister Turner had given evidence, counsel for the prosecution applied to the Judge for the evidence of a Leeds police officer, Detective Officer, W B Cairns, to be taken next. Counsel said that Detective Officer Cairns had to return to Leeds to give evidence in a case at the Assizes at Leeds. The Judge granted the application.

Detective Officer Cairns spoke about a search he made at the flat of Mr and Mrs Davies in Belmont Grove, Leeds, and said that he looked in a cavity in a coal cellar and saw a gold chain. When he pulled it out, he saw that two rings were fastened to it. Cross-examined, he said that the flat was searched thoroughly, but nothing else was found. There was also a thorough search at the Hotel Metropole by police officers, but as far as he knew nothing was found.

The manager of the Station Hotel, Stafford, Mr G L Farr, spoke of Green's visits to the hotel. On July 16 Green had lunch in the dining room with four other men, he said. After lunch, the four men went upstairs to the residents' lounge, but he did not see where Green went. When Green returned to the hotel in the evening, he told the witness that he had been across to the station and fell asleep on the platform.

When Mr Baker was pressing Mr Farr to state exactly what Green had said, the Judge remarked: "It is idle to pretend that anybody can repeat verbatim what was said so long ago, on July 16th, without notes."

Questioned about his evidence at the committal proceedings at Stone (Staffs.), Mr Farr agreed that he did not say, then that Green had told him that he fell asleep "on the platform." He (witness) inferred that Green had been asleep "on the platform."

Mr Baker: "Do you think you had gathered wrongly when you gathered that he had fallen asleep on the platform?"
"I don't think so".

Mr Farr said that an RAF-type mackintosh was inside the top of the bag Green was carrying.

Mr Farr also said that he noticed the mackintosh because he had formerly served in the RAF. When he was shown a brown mackintosh and asked if that was the coat he had seen on the top of Green's bag, he replied that it was not the one.

Mr Baker: "Did you have any conversation about the coat?"

Mr Farr: "No".

"I suggest you are mistaken about the coat?"

155

"The coat I saw was an RAF type"

.

Re-examined by Mr Richardson, Mr Farr said that in his first statement to the police, he spoke about the coat.

The Judge: "Is the position this, that you were the first to mention the coat?"
Mr Farr: "Yes".

Next Chief Inspector Edwin Holton, of the Fingerprints Branch, Scotland Yard, spoke of tests he had made of a footprint alleged to have been made by shoes found in the a hold-all at Green's home. He said the pattern could have been made by the shoes. He had reached that opinion as the result of tests, some of which he had made when he himself was wearing the shoes. Once, during chief Inspector Holton's evidence, the Judge left his seat to look more closely at photographs which the witness was using to demonstrate ridges made by the shoes on a piece of flooring taken from the kitchen at the Wiltshaw's home.

I was brought to the stand. I endeavoured to speak clearer for the Court, not using Leeds dialect.

Richardson: "Mr Blackburn has told us you offered to lend him some money:
Green: "I probably did but in a joking sort of manner."

Richardson: "Mr Blackburn said that you showed him some money in a wallet?"
Green: "That I do not remember. I rather think he saw money at the time I was buying some drinks. I do not distinctly remember taking out my wallet and showing him." I then added that the wallet was my own. I don't know why I said that as it just could

have been construed by the jury that it might not possibly have been mine, but I wanted to emphasise that it was mine.

I was then asked about the visit later that evening to the flat of Nurse Davies, who also worked at the Claremont Nursing Home, in Belmont Grove, Leeds.

Mr Baker: "Later still, did you go to the Claremont Nursing Home?"
Green: "Yes."
Mr Baker: "Who did you see there?"
Green: "I saw Sister Turner and another nurse, but I do not know who she was."

Mr Baker: "Do you remember what happened between you and Sister Turner that night?"
Green: "No it was just another visit to the nursing home."

Mr Baker: "Sister Turner has told us that you said your aunt had been murdered, you mentioned Mrs Wiltshaw's name and said you had been to see your uncle."
Green: "I did mention that to her, but whether it was that time I am not sure, or if those were the words I used."

Mr Baker: "Why did you refer to Mrs Wilshaw as your aunt?"
Green: "I had mentioned it in the Metropole Hotel, as I was staying there as Mr Wiltshaw, but whether I used the same words to Sister Turner I cannot say. I do remember saying that I had been down there that day."
Baker: "Had you been down there?"
Green: "No, sir."

I was then asked if it was true that I had a bandage on my wrist, and I said it probably was true.

Mr Baker: "Do you remember Sister Turner joking to you, saying that you would have to be careful as the police were looking for a man with scratches?"

Green: "Yes, and I used the expression, 'You will find scratches all over me' That was meant in a joking manner.".

Mr Baker: "Did you tell Sister Turner a story about your father having a pottery works and that you had two sisters, one of whom was a doctor?"
Green: "These were, I should say, her own deductions from what I had said over the period I had known her."

Mr Baker: "Sister Turner says you told her you were going to buy a bungalow for Nurse Lammey and yourself for £4,500?"

Green: "I dint say that."

Asked about the rings, I said that, on Thursday, July 17th, Miss Lammey had the rings. I thought she was wearing one of them but nothing was said or done about the rings as far as I can remember that night, though I knew that some remarks had been passed. The following day I had the rings back again.

Asked about the ring boxes, I replied. "On 17th July I spent the night at the Metropole and the following day met Miss Lammey in the afternoon. I had been to a Leeds jeweller's, M M Henderson Ltd, and bought two ring boxes. I thought I had offered the ring boxes to Miss Lammey, but found later that I still had them. In my possession."

Mr Baker: "Miss Lammey said she had had a letter from her sister in which it was stated that the police had been to the sister's home looking for a man named Leslie Green. What was the outcome of Miss Lammey receiving that letter."

158

Green: "I told Miss Lammey that I would go out and ring the Belfast police, but I dint do so.

Mr Baker: "So, where did you go to instead of making that call?"
Green: "I just needed to think and it was a way of getting Miss Lammey on side. However, later that day, Miss Lammey gave the rings back to me. She was not happy after seeing the letter from Ireland."

Mr Baker: "Tell me your movements that night."
Green: "Miss Lammey and I went to a theatre that night and I stayed the night at the Davies's flat. There was a time when we were both together in the flat, then Miss Lammey went home and I was there by myself. On Sunday, July 20, I had lunch at the flat with her. We spoke about the letter and I told her I would go to Stoke police if that would ease her mind but she told me she had also had a telephone call from her sister in Belfast, which upset her. That Sunday was the last time I was at the Davies' flat."

In reply to Mr Baker, I said I left the rings and gold chain in the small recess in the coal cellar at the flat.

Mr Baker: "But, from your police report, you said you have thrown the rings and boxes in the river?"
Green: "That wasn't true. Yes, I remember drawing a plan for Supt. Spooner of New Scotland Yard, purporting to show the position where I had thrown the property into the water. That wasn't true. I needed to put Supt Spooner on a false trail as I didn't want the police to go to Nurse Davies' flat."

Mr Baker: "What happened to the cigarette case and chain?"
Green: I sold them to a jeweller's shop in Vicar Lane, Leeds and got between £10 and £12 for them."

Mr Baker: "You never mentioned that in any of your police statements?"
Green: "No, sir."

Mr Baker asked me more questions about the Sunday night. I said it was about 8.45pm when I met Miss Lammey outside the nursing home. It was true that I had intended to get a train more than two hours before, and it was a surprise for her when I met her.

We went first to the Metropole and later I changed my mind about getting a train and we went to some gardens instead. When they closed we walked to some more gardens.

It was there that I decided to make a clean breast of everything to Miss Lammey. I was in too deep with all the lies I had concocted about being related to the Wiltshaws. The first thing I told her was that I had a criminal past and was a petty thief. I told her the story I had built up about being rich, being a member of the Wiltshaw family and having a traveller job in the pottery industry was completely made up, just to try to impress her. I then told her I had worked as a chauffeur/gardener to the Wiltshaws until I was sacked on 1st July for using their car to drive to Leeds to see her. Miss Lammey asked me if I had been involved in the robbery. I replied that I knew too much about the place to be able to do the robbery without having to commit murder.

I did tell Miss Lammey that I remembered discussing the Wiltshaw house with Charles and that it was loaded up with jewellery and antiques. I supposed Charles could have taken it into his head to do the robbery, but I didn't say to Miss Lammey that I thought he had done so. In my mind Charles and Lorenzo may well have robbed the place."

The Judge then interrupted: "Did you ever tell Miss Lammey that you were already married?"

Green: "No, sir, I didn't."

Answering further questions, I replied that Charles had asked him to do a housebreaking. He was referring then to the Wiltshaw's house, as we had been talking about it, but I backed out. I did not mention any other names other than Charles and Lorenzo.

Mr Baker:" So, what happened after the walk in the park?"
Green: "I walked Miss Lammey back to the nursing home and in the early hours caught a train to Torquay."

Mr Baker: "Why did you go to Torquay?"
Green: "There was no special reason for going to Torquay and I don't know why I chose Torquay. I just wanted to get away from Leeds and Stoke, just to relax and think. I'd told Miss Lammey I would go to the police, but I dint know what the outcome would be if I did so. I knew I would be brought in for questioning. I knew I had not done the Wiltshaw murder but wondered if I would be able to prove myself innocent. I had no real alibi for the time of the murder and I knew that things would not be too pleasant for Miss Lammey."

Well, I suppose I must have come to a decision and went to Shrewsbury. I rang Miss Lammey from theer and met her that night in Birmingham. I told her I had nothing to fear about going to the police and that I had been in Stafford on the day of the murder.

I went home to see me wife, but could not get in and slept in an outside building. The next morning I went to the police station.

The thing is on saying this, I remember I was dressed differently when I went to Longton Police Station. This must have been another blackout. I had no memory of actually seeing Constance, but I must have done as I'd changed clothes! Spooner must have

161

realised this and I saw him speaking to the defence counsel. I told myself I had to concentrate otherwise my case was lost.

Answering questions about a statement made to Sergeant Millen, of New Scotland Yard, referring to Miss Lammey, I said that I did not want Lorenzo and Charles to be involved.

After two hours and 50 minutes my examination-in-chief ended. Mr Justice Stable asked me if I would like a five-minute break before cross-examination began. I replied, "No, my lord, I would prefer to go straight on."

In reply to Mr Ryder Richardson, I said that I had made two visits to Miss Lammey in Ireland, returning after the second with her.

Mr Richardson summed up my movements. So, Green, on July 10th you booked in at the Metropole, Leeds, and stayed in the city until July 13th. You went to London on July 14th, were in Stafford on July 16th and Leeds in the early hours of July 17th. You remained in Leeds until July 20th. On July 21st you were in Birmingham, July 22nd at Longton, near Stafford and on July 23rd you went to the police. Is that correct?"

Green: I am not going to tie myself to any dates sithee, because I have neither a photographic memory nor an infallible memory.

You do not have to, we have your memory mapped out here.

Mr Baker took over: "First of all, you made a long statement to the police in which you dealt in considerable detail with your visit to Ireland with Nora Lammey and how you met her?"

"Yes, sir."

Mr Baker: "Is that account substantially accurate?"

"Substantially."

Then followed details questioning about the state of my finances, during which I admitted that, while staying at the Strand Palace Hotel, I had stolen a purse from a handbag, which had been left unattended. "There was £15 in it.

The RAF raincoat that Mr Wiltshaw had recognised as his own was then produced. We heard that it had been found in the left luggage at Holyhead.

Mr Baker: "Do you remember ever seeing this raincoat?"
"No, sir." I replied stoutly, "I have never seen it before. I also have never had the mackintosh in my possession."

Mr Richardson then returned for more questioning: You state that Lorenzo and Charles gave you money, can you tell the Court the reasoning behind this obvious generosity on their part?"

I couldn't think quickly, and mumbled something like, "Lorenzo was hoping that I would help him in some criminal enterprise.

Mr Richardson: I am suggesting to you that you are rather an accomplished liar?

Green: I have told lies.

Richardson: It is not more than that. All through this case we have come across person after person to whom you have told lies?"
Green: I have told some but, I am not a persistent liar.

Mr Justice Stable suggested that the word persistent" be substituted for "accomplished."

Mr Ryder Richardson: Is it not true when you lie about a fact you must not give too much detail because that might lead to the discovery of your lie?

Green: "I suppose so."

Richardson: "Just as an example – would you not have found it difficult if someone to whom you were posing as Mr Wiltshaw had asked you where your father lived when he was a boy?"

Green: "I have never posed to anyone as Mr Wiltshaw."

Richardson: "I suggest that that is another lie. Take care, you are on oath. You did pose as Terry Wiltshaw at the Hotel metropole in Leeds?"

"Green: "Only in name."

Richardson: "How else does one pose?"

Green: "I was only using the name and address on the visitors' book."

Richardson then asked where I got the money from to travel by air to Ireland.

Green: "I admit to borrowing £13 from Miss Lammey."

Richardson: "What I am suggesting is that until July 16th you were short of money, after July 16th you had plenty?"

Green: "I had been involved in various criminal activities, which involved stealing, and I always had brass in me pocket. I did not borrow from Nurse Lammey as long as I had money. I believe that, on the last Saturday I spent in Leeds, I had about £10-15."

Richardson: "Then by Sunday midday, 13th July, you had rather less than £10-£15"
Green: "Yes."

Mr Justice Stable interrupted once again, with a bluntness that was by now beginning to seem familiar to the Court: "Green, let us get down to brass tacks about this. You told us that it was untrue that you had your wallet stolen or lost with £40 in it. You are saying that, by Sunday morning, the 13th, however much money you had, it had all be stolen. Had none been stolen?"

Green: "No, sir."

Justice Stable: "You were prepared to borrow money from Nurse Lammey and others while you had enough money to pay your hotel bill?"
Green: "Yes, because I was strapped - I needed the money."

Richardson: "Did you obtain any other money?"
Green: "No, sir."

Richardson: "It was quite false you had lost £40?"
Green: "No, sir. It was quite true." *I was getting quite flummoxed now. Richardson was badgering me, asking the same question over and over, but phrased differently, and I didn't know what I was saying.*

Richardson posed the same question: "Just to clarify. You have said you had £10-15 and that you acquired no further money. Did you lose £40?"
Green: "It was untrue to say that I did."

165

Richardson: "So, I presume you did not have the £40 to lose?"
Green: "No, sir."

Richardson: "On Sunday you were trying to borrow, pretending that something had happened when it had not?"
Green: "Yes."

Richardson: "On the Sunday you were in desperate straits for money?"
Green: Not desperate straits – I just had this hotel bill to pay."

The Judge: "You have told the jury you had your wallet lost or stolen with £40 in it."
Green: "There were one or two pounds in it."

Council for Defence: "You were willing to lie to borrow money to pay an hotel bill?
Green: "Yes, sir".

Council: "It was clear that either you would have to work or acquire money quickly?"
Green: "Yes."

Council (changing the subject): "You had seen Mrs Wiltshaw wearing valuable jewellery on many occasions?"
Green: "Outside the brooch and rings, I did not see any other jewellery."

Council: "You knew Mrs Wiltshaw had jewellery that was valuable?"
Green: "'Appen so. As like as mebbee."

Council: "Between 5 and 5.30pm she would be alone in the house?"
Green: "Yes".

Council: "You knew if she saw you in the act of stealing, she would have to be silenced?"
Green: It is an obvious fact."

Council: "You knew if you went to that house that you would have to wear gloves?"
Green: If I took part in any criminal activity I should have to wear gloves."

Council: "You knew there was a poker in the grate?"
Green: "Yes, sir."

At this point I was handed a poker with an iron barb near the end of it. I held it for a few moments and then passed it back to a police officer.

Richardson: "You did go to that house that day, Green?"
Green: "No sir". (Richardson was intimidating me, with a raised voice.)

Richardson (almost shouting): "You killed Mrs Wiltshaw?"
Green: (I was beginning to shake and just about managed to get the words out) "No, sir" I could see the people in the crowded Assize Court leaning forward to try to hear me.

The Judge: "Can the accused please speak up."

So, I tried again, trying to put more stress into my answer, "NO, SIR." I managed to reply, this time louder.

Richardson then asked me a number of questions about the shoes found in my bag and suggested that they were foreign-made ones. I replied that I had bought them from someone in Manchester.

Richardson: "It is quite clear that the person who went to that house went to it in the only hour in the 24 when the jewellery was protected by one person. Is that coincidence?"

Green: "I don't see any connection."

Richardson: "If you don't know the whereabouts of jewellery, you have to make a rapid search?"
Green: "Never having gone in for that sort of thing. I would not know."

That was a silly thing to say – of course I'd done house-breaking, having to make rapid searches, and they knew that. I'm just building a bigger hole for myself!

I was then asked questions about the cut on my thumb and the cut on the thumb of the glove found in the garden at the Wiltshaws' home after the murder.

Richardson: "You have been noted to have said that the police have lied and the evidence has been rigged?"
Green: "Evidence was given by Mr Arthur that he saw a mark on my thumb. That was quite untrue. The thumb of the glove was cut so it would coincide with the mark on my thumb."

Richardson: "Are you saying that Professor Webster did something deliberately dishonest?"
Green: "Yes, sir".

Richardson: "So, you are saying Dr Arthur has come here to give perjured evidence?"
Green: "Evidence by Dr Arthur about the mark on my thumb is a lie."

Richardson: "What about Supt Lockley? Is that a lie?"

168

Green: "Yes, sir. Supt Lockley saw the marks on my hand and arm, but he did not point out the cut on my left thumb." *I was desperate to clear myself in some way. I had no memory of going to the Wiltshaw's and all I could think of was they had their man and had planted evidence on me to prove it. Of course, no-one was going to believe me.*

The Judge: "Did you make any protest at the time that you thought this matter was being improperly handled."
Green: "No sir."

Richardson: You claim to have caught an earlier train on the 16th than the one on which the RAF coat was found. A ticket collector has given evidence that he spoke to you at 7.20pm – nearly 15 minutes after that train's departure, so how could you have been on an earlier train?"
Green: That ticket collector was also mistaken."

Richardson: You state he was mistaken, although the Station Hotel manager said you would miss the 7.07pm train if you were staying for dinner, but would be in time for the 7.50pm train.

Green: I just had some snap. I didn't stay for the full meal, and caught the 7.07pm train.

Richardson: "Changing the subject. You had a sports coat?"
Green: "Yes."

Richardson: "What happened to it?"
Green: "I gave it to Lorenzo."

Richardson: "So there was no chance this coat could have been covered in blood and you disposed of it"

Green: "I was not at the Wiltshaw house. I did not do the murder.

Richardson then mentioned the cigarette case that Mr Bleasby, a porter at the Hotel Metropole saw on July 17th.

Green: Mr Bleasby was mistaken when he said that I had a gold cigarette case.

Richardson then asked how I would know I was going to be welcome at 1am on July 17th at the nursing home.
Green: I knew I would be welcomed, but the nursing home was closed, so I got through the window of the nurses' sitting room and Nurse Finchley was mistaken when she said she let me in at the door. Sister Turner was also mistaken when she said she saw me come in through the door.

I was getting so muddled up now with dates. My mind was a turmoil. I don't know if I was getting mixed up letting myself in through the window on Sunday 20th.

I was then asked if I had the rings on me at that time.
Green: "I did not have the rings on me then so Sister Turner couldn't have seen one on my finger."

Counsel: "You say you received from Lorenzo two rings: did you recognise them as the rings Mrs Wiltshaw had worn?"
Green: "No, sir."

Richardson: "Why did you not ring up the police in Belfast?"
Green: "I don't know."

Richardson: "When did you hide the rings in Mrs Davies's flat?"
Green: "On the Sunday."

Richardson: "You put them in a place where you could get them again when the storm blew over?"

Green: "Yes."

Richardson: "Did you not think about Mrs and Mrs Davies's comfort when you hid them?"
Green: "No."

Richardson: "Why did you tell the police you had thrown these rings into the canal?"
Green: "To mislead them."

Judge: "When you hid this property in Mrs Davies's flat, had you a shrew idea that it had been stolen from the Wiltshaw's?"
Green: "I had an idea."

Richardson: "You were pretending to Miss Lammey that you were anxious to go to the police?"
Green: "Yes."

Richardson: "Did you mention the name of Charles in connection with this crime?"
Green: "Yes."

Richardson: "On Monday, July 21st, would it be fair to say that the state of your mind was such you could not stay in any one place?
Green: "I could have done if I had wanted."

Richardson: "You told Miss Lammey you were going to Stoke?"
Green: "Yes."

Richardson: "You also told Miss Lammey you were going to Torquay?"
Green: "Yes."

At this time the Judge adjourned the trial until the next day. "We will continue with Green's evidence tomorrow."

Chapter 22

Day 4, – December 4th, 1952

Immediately the last of the prosecution witnesses had given evidence, Mr G G Baker, QC, (for Green) announced his intention of calling his client.

I was being questioned about the bruise I sustained in the fall, on the stone steps, while out walking.

I decided to unfasten the cuff of my shirt, turned to members of the jury seated just behind me, lifted up my right arm and showed them a mark on my wrist. I told the jury that the mark had been caused some weeks before the day of the murder, July 16th, when I fell down some steps on Ilkley Moor.

Answering further questions, I told of meeting two men in Leeds, Lorenzo and Charles. I said I did not know their surnames. Lorenzo had given me two rings, which I found out later were the same rings the prosecution alleged are part of the jewellery, worth £3,000, stolen from the home of Mrs Wiltshaw.

I also said that Lorenzo had given me a few "bits of gold" and a gold cigarette case. I had sold the cigarette case and a gold chain in the jeweller's shop in Vicar Lane."

(Up to the last few hours of the trial, the police were working to strengthen their case. Minutes after Green had stated in evidence that he had sold a gold cigarette case in a Leeds jeweller's shop in Vicar Lane, a message was sent to Leeds CID asking them to check the story and, if possible, find the case.)

Asked how I knew Lorenzo, I explained that our first meeting was at the Cameo Ballroom, Longton (Staffs) where I had formerly had a part-time job as a cloakroom attendant. Lorenzo had approached me there and said he remembered that they were in the same cell at Durham Prison some years ago.

I acknowledged that Lorenzo was also a petty thief as we had discussed breaking and entering proposals made by Lorenzo and I said that we once went to Huddersfield together in Lorenzo's car to do a warehouse job, but it did not come off.

After the lunch adjournment, replying to Mr Richardson, I said that I was hoping to get money from Lorenzo.

Richardson: "So, either he or thefts were your only source of money at that time?"
Green: "Yes, sir."

Richardson: "No question of Charles giving you money or jewellery?"
Green: "No, sir."

Richardson: "It's a strange relationship, not knowing much about this Lorenzo. I mean, you didn't even know his first name. Why did you not ask him questions about himself?"
Green: "I just didn't."

Richardson: "You had a good deal of association with motor cars. What was the registration number of Lorenzo's car?"
Green: "I haven't got the foggiest idea."

Judge: "Is this right? You did not know the number of his car, nor where he lived, not his address, nor the town?"

Green: I had no idea. I think he lived in Leeds."

Oh God, I was thinking, this is just going to make them think that Lorenzo and Charlie don't even exist and I've made them up. All these questions – my mind has gone blank, why can't I remember?

Anyway, the questioning continued. I said that Lorenzo had given me two rings in ring boxes but I threw the cases away. I said I couldn't remember where exactly, but it was somewhere in Leeds.

Asked about meeting up with Lorenzo, I said I had made an arrangement to meet him and Charles in Spinks's Bar, in Leeds, some weeks before but they didn't turn up.

Richardson: "Where had that arrangement been made?"
Green: "I don't remember but it was abart two weeks afore the 17th."

Then Mr Richardson said: "I am going to suggest that neither Lorenzo nor Charles existed, they were, in fact, myths."

Yes, out in the open now – all because of my stupid memory and not paying attention – so they do think I've just made them up! I could hear Terry in the back of my head, but I didn't want to listen to him. It was him who got me into all this mess in the first place.

Finally, Counsel for the prosecution referred to the 'old-fashioned poker' with which the prosecution alleged the murder had been committed. "Did you tell Nurse Davies that Mrs Wiltshaw had been killed by an old-fashioned poker?" Richardson asked.
"I don't remember that."

"Nurse Davies said that you did." Shot back Ryder Richardson. "How did you know Mrs Wiltshaw had been killed with a poker like that?"

"If I did say that, I must have read about it in the paper", was the reply.

"Which paper?" Ryder Richardson snapped.
Green: "Either the Daily Mail or Daily Express."
Richardson: "I suggest you cannot find any newspaper in which the description of an old-fashioned poker is given prior to July 19th or 20th?"

Yet again, the judge leaned over to make a point, "Think carefully over the question – take all the time you want."

I just couldn't think straight with all these questions being bombarded at me. My head started hurting but I had to say something. They were all looking at me, wanting an answer. I wanted to run, but I couldn't, I had to stand there. I felt humiliated.

When I could only repeat that I had "read of the poker in the newspaper," four copies, two of each newspaper, morning papers for 17th and 18th July were brought into the court and scanned closely by the judge and the accused. Finally, it was clear that no mention had even made of the fact that Mrs Wilshaw was killed by a poker, although one paper did say that the dead woman had used to poker to defend herself. Nowhere was the phrase 'old-fashioned' used.

I was again asked "Did you kill Mrs Wiltshaw?"

I replied quietly but firmly: "No, sir."

Then I was asked: "Were you at the Wiltshaw house at all on July 16th?"

"No, sir."

"Did you steal any of these rings or jewellery or the cigarette case?"
"No, sir."

"Did you go to Barlaston at all on Wednesday, July 16th?
"No, sir".

I said that I had told Superintendent R Spooner, of Scotland Yard, that I had thrown some jewellery into the water from a bridge near the Golden Lion Hotel, Leeds, in an effort to mislead him. Actually I had hidden the jewellery in a flat in Belmont Grove, Leeds.

It was the turn of Mr Baker, defending counsel. He pointed out that none of the other jewellery missing from Estoril had turned up or had been traced to the prisoner. He also complained that the prosecution had not called the four men who had been in the Station Hotel with Green. He had to admit that Green himself had said that the evidence pointed to him and it would be foolish to try to gainsay the matter. He reminded the jury that three women had inspected an identity parade of eleven men and two had failed. The other had only picked out Green at the second attempt and, while it could not be denied that Green knew the Wiltshaws and was familiar with Estoril, this surely pointed away from him as the perpetrator of the crime. "If he has anything, he has sense, he was going to be very chary about going back to the place from where he had been dismissed."

Dealing with the marks on the kitchen floor, Baker complained that the evidence of the Scotland Yard officer had not differentiated between sole and heel. All he could say was that the spaces between the ridges were about the same. There were many people milling about in the kitchen that afternoon and no evidence of elimination had been presented to the court. The marks could have been left by anybody wearing similar shoes. A telling point was that no trace of pottery fragments or bloodstains had been

177

found on the shoes and when Green returned to the Station Hotel, he was in no way distressed or ruffled, as one might expect from the man who had just committed an horrific murder.

I thought, "OK, I've got a chance – Baker's pointed out that I wasn't covered in blood and there was no sign of blood on my shoes or pottery fragments. Surely the jury with recognise I couldn't have been there!"

His final sentence was in the form of a question to the accused man, "Did you have any part in the killing" "No, sir", was my reply.

During my cross-examination, in reply to one question, I said: "I know I did not do the crime myself, but the evidence which has come out – whether it is coincidence or not – would, I agree, to a certain extent, point to me. I have now been in custody five months on this charge and, quite honestly, I have lost any feelings about it."

I was then asked: "You don't care if you are convicted or not?" I replied quietly: "I would not say that."

At that moment a number of police officers, including Chief Detective-Superintendent Thomas Lockley, approached Mr Ryder Richardson. Mr Richardson approached the judge. I heard him say that he was expecting some information that was vital to the case. The Judge left the courthouse with Mr Richardson and Mr Baker, for about quarter of an hour.

After this time, they returned. The hearing was resumed immediately. Mr Richardson, who had been cross-examining me, then announced that he had no further questions to put to me.

Nothing had been said about the delay, but I noticed some time later that a Leeds detective officer, who had previously given evidence in the case, was among the police officers in court.

I was the only witness called by the defence and counsel then addressed the jury.

Mr Ryder Richardson made it quite clear to the jury that the case for the prosecution had been proved beyond any question of doubt.

Mr Richardson had finished his speech and Mr Baker had been speaking for nearly an hour and a half when the Court was adjourned for the day.

The afternoon was now drawing on and the judge intimated that he would start his summing up on the next morning after final speeches from counsel.

Before adjourning, the Judge spoke, "Tomorrow it is expected that Mr Baker will speak for about an hour and I will start my summing-up, which it is expected will take three hours or more. The verdict is expected late tomorrow afternoon."

I left the witness-box after giving evidence, altogether I must have been on that stand for about five and a half hours.

. . . .

It was only then I realised that I should have said I had seen the poker many a time, having made up the fire on numerous occasions – but I'd

179

lost my chance. I'd been so flummoxed by all the questions and I was so tired I couldn't think straight. Stupid me, saying I'd seen the description of the poker, as being an old-fashioned poker, in a newspaper. Would I have another chance? My defence should have picked that up. If only I'd listened to Terry, maybe he would have had the memory of Lorenzo's car and reminded me about the poker.

Chapter 23

Day 5, Friday, 5th December 1952

Shortly after the hearing began this morning, a large queue, composed mainly of women, formed outside the court in the hope of getting seats for this afternoon's hearing.

The summing-up began at 11.25am. Earlier, Mr G G Baker, QC, defending, had told members of the jury that they had seen what sort of fellow Green was.

"Was he the beast who was in Estoril that evening?" he asked.
You have all gained an idea of what Green is like over the court of this trial. Yes, Green is a "thief, a rotter and blackguard, which he has admitted himself, but not a murderer.

The prosecution has alleged that Green murdered Mrs Wiltshaw, wife of a wealthy pottery manufacturer, and stole jewellery from her home. Green has denied the allegations and has said that he was not at Estoril on the day of the murder and had in fact been asleep on a bench in Stafford, after a heavy lunch with alcohol.

Green may well have received two rings and a gold cigarette case from Lorenzo and Charles but not committed the robbery or murder himself. As you will have heard, Superintendent Spooner, of Scotland Yard, had stated that he had made a search in Leeds for a Lorenzo and Charles, but was unable to find them. To my mind the word would have got round that one of the 'Big Five' was in the city, and underworld characters would have no desire to show themselves. This, I suggest, may have been why Superintendent Spooner was not able to trace the two.

Green sold the case and it was quite reasonable that a man of Green's criminal past would have tried to hide two valuable rings until the 'heat went off' and he could return to them. I suggest that may account for the finding of the two rings in a cavity in the coal cellar at the Belmont Grove, Leeds, flat of Nurse Davies. Green had also sold the gold cigarette case in a Leeds jeweller's shop.

I reiterate that Green had been receiving the stolen property, but that was no reason for thinking that, because the jewellery was in his possession, he had committed the murder. I point out to you, the jury, that the two rings and the case were only a small part of the jewellery missing from Estoril, none of which had been found, despite a very careful police search.

I also wish to bring to the jury's attention that the prosecution had not called the four men who had been in the Station Hotel with Green. I have to admit that Green himself has said that the evidence points to him and it would be foolish to try to gainsay the matter, but I remind the jury that three women had inspected an identity parade of eleven men and two had failed. The other had only picked out Green at the second attempt and, while it could not be denied that Green knew the Wiltshaws and was familiar with Estoril, this surely pointed away from him as the perpetrator of the crime.

Now I come to the marks on the kitchen floor. I hereby make a complaint that the evidence of the Scotland Yard officer had not differentiated between sole and heel. All he could say was that the spaces between the ridges were about the same. There were many people milling about in the kitchen that afternoon and no evidence of elimination has been presented to the court. The marks could have been left by anybody wearing similar shoes.

I wish also to state, for the record, and bring to the jurors' attention to the telling point that no trace of pottery fragments or bloodstains had been found on the shoes and, when Green returned to the Station Hotel, he was in no way distressed or ruffled, as one might expect from a man who had just committed an horrific murder. I ask you, how could a man who had hammered a woman senseless and to a pulp, and run a poker through her, go back and calmly eat his dinner?"

I also believe it was impossible for Green, after last being seen at the hotel in Stafford, where he dined, to have caught a train to Barlaston, get to Estoril, carry out the murder and robbery, get back to Barlaston Station and then be seen at Stafford Hotel at the time he was seen. It would have been nigh impossible in my view. Mrs Wiltshaw was last seen at 5.15pm on July 16th. At 5.25, the chauffeur-gardener now employed there left. Mr Wiltshaw returned home at 6.20pm. There was nothing to prove what time the murder was actually committed.

All the other evidence you have heard has been circumstantial and I ask you to bear that in mind when coming to your decision."

Mr Baker then address me, "Did you have any part in the killing?" "No", I replied firmly.

Mr Baker completed his final submissions for the defence on the morning of 5th December by admitting that, "The murder was possibly unparalleled in its bestiality."

"Hell fire," I thought to myself. "That was my defence! That was probably the worst thing that he could have said to the jury – just leave them with the ghastly impression that the 'murder was possibly unparalleled in its bestiality!' I've no chance now."

The prosecuting counsel went into long detail about the case.

Richardson addressed the jury. "Well, members of the jury, you have heard over the past five days about the movements and actions of the defendant, which I will endeavour to sum up.

Green had made a long statement to the police about his movements before and after the murder, but we are concerned with the events of the actual day in question,

Green arrived at Stafford on July 16th and went to the Station Hotel. He had lunch, which he finished about 3.30pm and, so far as the prosecution could say, he was next in the hotel about 6.30 or 6.35pm.

The manager saw him about 3.30pm and the next time he saw him was when he came up the steps of the hotel at about 6.35pm, carrying a bag."

Mr Richardson went on: "If the prosecution is right, you will probably think he had plenty of time to go 10 miles or so to commit murder and come back. He would not want to get there before 5.30pm and he would want to have left as soon as his objective was achieved."

"The hotel manager noticed that, on the top of his bag, was an RAF-type raincoat. Green asked the time of the evening meal and then discussed the time of the trains to Leeds. Green had his meal, left the hotel and went to the railway station where he had a conversation with the ticket collector.

He arrived in Leeds at the Hotel Metropole about 12.30am. A porter booked him in and Green offered him money to pay the bill he owed.

Green went to the nursing home where Miss Lammey worked, and there he showed two beautiful rings to Nurse Turner, who worked with her.

I submit that these were Mrs Wiltshaw's rings, undoubtedly stolen at the time the murder was committed.

Next day Green paid his hotel bill and that evening met Miss Lammey and gave her two rings. He was introduced to Nurse Davies, who worked at the same nursing home, and who lived with her husband in a flat in Belmont Road, Leeds.

They gave her and Green permission to stay at their flat on July 18th and 19th. This is where the two rings and a gold chain were found, hidden in a coal cellar.

Green went to a jeweller's shop, bought two ring cases and suggested to Miss Lammey that she should put the rings in them. But, by this time she was so disturbed that she returned the rings to him.

Mr Richardson continued, "Tests made by the police showed that the cuts on the wash-leather glove coincided with a cut on Green's thumb. The way in which the glove and the cut fitted was, in the opinion of the prosecution, a damning piece of evidence.

As to the RAF-type mackintosh, which the railway police managed to discover in a left luggage office, it had blood on the inside of the right sleeve of the same group as Green's. Also, as we have heard from the railway police, a ticket was bought for the same train that the mackintosh was discovered – a ticket bought at Barlaston, going through to Leeds. You may think this is circumstantial evidence but I ask the jury to bear this in mind when coming to your verdict.

I put to you also that a pair of shoes, found to be in Green's possession, when he presented himself at Longton Police Station, may also have had blood on them, but had been washed off."

There was a general murmur in the audience at this statement.

The judge brought his gavel down and called "Order in Court".

I was astounded. How could I possibly have blood on my shoes? I was never there? The jury will now just get the impression there had been signs of blood. This is the end of me!

There was an objection to this by Baker. "My Lord, this is pure speculation. No blood has been found on the shoes."

Judge: "Sustained. The jury will ignore the last statement by Mr Richardson."

Mr Richardson resumed, "I apologise my Lord. However, the soles of these shoes, when subjected to tests, made marks similar to those found on the kitchen floor at the Wiltshaws' home. The same flooring you, the jury, have seen.

Therefore, as the case has been presented to you, even though Green has at all times denied that he was the author of the crime, there is no doubt in my mind that that the weight of circumstantial evidence is so great that there could be no reasonable doubt that Green committed the murder and robbery."

That's when I started scratching in the witness stand the words, "Leslie Green's last stand." It was all over bar the judge's summing up.

Listening in, Terry was astounded, saying to himself, "I did clean those shoes thoroughly! So, that's the end of me, Leslie and Terrance. There's no coming back from this."

P C Dobson was standing by thinking all the work he had done to bring the culprit to trail, the questioning, the posters, the searches, had finally paid off. Green was going to hang.

………………

The Judge continued his summing-up after lunch, following an hour and 35 minutes before lunch. The judge left his red-canopied chair and went to the end of the Bench, sitting next to the members of the jury, not more than a yard from the jury box, in order that the rumbling of traffic on the nearby arterial road should not prevent them from hearing him.

"Mr Baker said that Sup Spooner of Scotland Yard had stated that he made a search in Leeds for a Lorenzo and Charles, but was unable to find them, although word may have got around and they have since disappeared.

Green had been receiving the stolen property, but that was no reason for thinking that, because the jewellery was in his possession, he had committed the murder. He pointed out that the two rings and the case were only a small part of the jewellery missing from Estoril, none of which had been found despite a very careful police search. There was nothing to prove what time the murder was committed.

Mr E Ryder Richardson, said the case against Green was circumstantial but, paraphrasing his own words, 'There was such a weight of evidence that there could be no reasonable doubt as to his guilt'."

187

Terry was in my head. "That was leading the jury! A judge in his summing up, shouldn't lead the jury. He's basically putting it on a plate that you are guilty and the jury should come to a guilty verdict."

Mr Justice Stable, continued in his summing-up, telling the jury not to be influenced in any way by the fact that Green was a self-confessed liar, nor should they allow their judgement to be prejudiced by the man's highly discreditable aims.

They should consider whether there was any truth in the story of the acquisition of the rings from Lorenzo and Charles.

The evidence falls under two headings: the time and means and the source from which Green obtained Mrs Wiltshaw's rings.

It has not been suggested that Green went to the house for the purpose of murdering Mrs Wiltshaw, but that he was surprised by her and, as he would immediately be recognised either he had to abandon his object of going for the jewellery or silence her forever.

Whoever it was at Estoril that day made certain that the woman would never be able to say who attacked her.

If Green had committed the murder, he must have gone from Stafford to Estoril in some way. There was no evidence about how that man, if he was the man, had been transported there and back. There could be no doubt, however, that whoever it was stole the jewellery, murdered Mrs Wiltshaw."

The inference was irresistible that the thief was also the murderer.

"Green stole in order to live a life of ease.

Timing was also of the essence, and if the jury accept those put forward by the prosecution, Green would have had two and a half hours to get from Stafford to Barlaston, commit the crime and return to Stafford. During all that time no-one appeared to have seen him, nor was there anyone who could substantiate Green's own story of the snooze in the park.

Where there is a conflict of evidence, jurors, I urge you to accept the construction most favourable to the prisoner. The burden of proof lies with the prosecution and you, the jury, cannot bring in a verdict of guilty unless you are all fully satisfied, after reviewing the whole of the evidence. If, on the other hand, you the jury are satisfied that the accused is guilty, you should do your duty.

Often taking off his spectacles and pointing them as he emphasised some particular matter, the Judge spoke for three hours and 25 minutes.

Just before 4 o'clock, the jury went out to consider their verdict, taking with them the bloodstained gloves found in the garden at the Wiltshaws' home, copies of the statements Green had made, photographs, and other exhibits.

Just 29 minutes later, I saw the jurors streaming back into the courtroom. 29 minutes – that meant they had all come to a quick decision, and I was done for. The jury usher, a police officer wearing white gloves and carrying a white wand, came through a green baize door leading to the Bench and whispered to the Judge's Clerk that the jury were agreed.

The jurors, including two women, filed into their places. Asked by the Clerk of Assize if they were agreed on their verdict, the foreman answered: "We are" and added "Guilty."

The three prison officers in the dock moved closer to me. I was looking straight ahead trying desperately to keep control. I knew I hadn't stood a chance with all the evidence against me, but I had been keeping a grip on the merest chance that the jury would decide there was no real proof. That grip had failed. I had no more chances to fight for my life.

When asked if I had anything to say, I somehow managed to reply with a firm voice: "No, my lord," The blood had rushed from my head and I felt myself come out in a cold sweat. I grasped the front of the dock to stop myself keeling over but then regained my composure, took my military stance.

The Chaplain placed the Black Cap on the Judge's head, and slowly, clearly and unhurriedly, Mr Justice Stable passed sentence of death.

I was led from the dock, walking firmly, looking neither right nor left, walked quickly down the steps to the cells. I was trying to blank everything out of my mind, the court, the jury, the judge, the spectators. Just one thought ran through my head that I'd never see my Nora again.

Reported by the Stafford correspondent of the Yorkshire Post:

After Green had left the dock, the Judge told the jury that they had discharged their duties admirably.

He asked Mr Baker if Green had been represented under the legal aid scheme, and Mr Baker said that was so. The Judge then remarked that nobody could have exerted himself more manfully than Mr Baker had done, or done it better.

"It is quite clear a very good job of work has been done by the police force," the Judge added.

Mr Ryder-Richardson, QC (for the Crown), said that it had been a tremendous task, and he had seen the results of some of the work. A thousand places were examined in one town alone.

The Judge: Is it true that, since this case stated you have found the cigarette case?

Mr Richardson: That is so. Leeds detectives visited shop after shop in the centre of the city – and the case was found. It had been sold by Green on the day that he said, but not with the gold chain. It had been in a fictitious name and address that Green had given for the jewellers. It was also noted that he had tried to sell jewellery at a shop in Bridge Street, Newcastle.

That was the vital information the prosecution were expecting when the trial was adjourned on Thursday and counsel went for a private consultation with the Judge in his private room,

Some people waited for nearly six hours to get to the public gallery to hear the closing stages of the trial. Many had brought flasks of hot tea and sandwiches

Chapter 24

The Yorkshire Post and Leeds Mercury, Wednesday, December 10, 1952

Green execution date:
The execution of Leslie Green, 29-year-old unemployed chauffeur, who was sentenced to death at Stafford assizes last Friday, for the murder of his former employer, Mrs Alice Maud May Wiltshaw, has been provisionally fixed for December 23, at Winson Green Prison, Birmingham.

....

In the eighteen days between sentence and execution, I occupied myself by reading to try to keep my thoughts from the hangman's noose. I read 'A Son of the People' by Baroness Orczy, 'A Life of Hopalong Cassidy' and H.V. Morton's 'Through the Lands of the Bible'. I think my body was winding down as I had nothing to keep alive for, just that silent walk to the noose. I began to suffer first of all with a bad cold, which the gaolers only gave me one handkerchief, with which to wipe my streaming nose, That was soon wet and soggy and I had to resort to my sleeve and shirt tail, which I tore a piece from. Then I began to suffer from toothache and had to have it extracted by the prison dentists.

I remained in touch with Nora Lammey and wrote asking her to send me some postage stamps as I was only allowed one official stamp per week.

My hopes for a reprieve were dashed by a letter dated 20th December 1952, from the Home Secretary, stating that there was no reason to interfere with the due process of the law.

I was miserable, cold and depressed and I still couldn't work out how my shoes got blood on them. I was so confused I was mixing up what was actually said and what was implied by Richardson. Did the prosecution actually put those shoes into the blood on the kitchen floor? I wouldn't put it past them, especially as nothing was mentioned about blood on the shoes when I first handed them over. Still, what was the point in going over and over the court decision? The jury had found me guilty. I had tried to say that I thought the evidence had been tampered with, but what was the point, as that was just seen as me being caught in a corner and trying to fight back with anything I could. No-one was going to refute the evidence of a learned doctor and the police.

As for the RAF-type mackintosh – well, I've no idea how that came into my possession. Maybe the person who did the murder, saw me asleep at Stafford, and put it on top of my bag. Oh, but that was just surmising, with no proof. It was all too late anyway, too very late.

Then I started thinking – what if I was there, but had wiped it from my memory because of the atrocity of the murder. These things happen. You hear of people losing their memory, with no idea of where they had been or even what their name is – normally happening after an atrocious experience that the brain couldn't handle. So, did I do the murder? I had had so many experiences of not remembering what I had done, where I had been, waking up to find myself elsewhere and not knowing how I got there, with this voice in my head telling me to do things and what to say. Maybe this voice in my head took control of me and made me murder poor Mrs Wiltshaw? But, surely it couldn't have made me kill. They say a hypnotist can make you do things and you have no recollection of doing them, but they can't make you do things that is innately abhorrent to the subject. If you're hypnotised to kill, somehow or other the subject would react and wake up. No, I couldn't have killed her.

I couldn't think any more, my brain hurt and I was ill, so I lay down on the prison bed and fell asleep.

.....

Terry sat up, feeling miserable too. The game was up, the dice was thrown and we'd lost. If only Leslie had given me a chance.

Still, it's probably a good idea that Leslie can't remember what actually happened.

I'd taken over when Leslie had gone to sleep on that bench. I saw Lorenzo and Charlie coming to catch the train to Barlaston.

"I've changed my mind, I will go with you." I shouted out to them.

So, we all got on the train together, but sitting separately, different compartments. That was the plan, just in case someone remembered three lads together.

Getting to the house, I went in first. The others were going to stay behind until I said the coast was clear. The little pooch didn't bark because he knew me and actually wagged his tail. I was hoping that Mrs Wiltshaw would be in the sitting room but she was in the kitchen preparing food for their evening meal.

"Terrance Leslie Green" she shouted out in annoyance and confusion. What are you doing here? You've no right. Go away, and she picked up a carving knife to shoo me away with it.

Hearing the name 'Terrance' was all that was needed for Terrance to show his face. He seemed to grow in stature, tower over the poor lady – from his now grotesque face came a growl. Mrs Wiltshaw screamed and in the same second threw a pan boiling

194

water holding potatoes at Terrance, complete with pan, which hit him over the head. He was enraged now, and there was no stopping him. I couldn't control him. His defence and fight mechanism turned on and the battering onslaught started, leaving her for dead. He also gave a dreadful kick to the poor pooch, kicking it, whimpering, out into the garden.

I ran upstairs to get the jewels, but heard movement going on downstairs, so ran down again. She had managed to get into the hall, leaving bloody hand prints in the door frame leading from the kitchen to the hall. Mrs Wiltshaw was trying to struggle to her feet. Terrance started throwing anything at her that was in arms reach, blocks of wood mainly then his eye rested on a hammer, which for some reason or other had been left in the hallway, aiming at her with it. Mrs Wiltshaw, in her weakened state and half blinded, made a vain attempt to defend herself, by seizing the poker by the fire in the hallway and waving it valiantly before her. This was just a final defiant gesture. Terrance just seized the poker and dreadfully mutilated the poor woman until she was well and truly dead.

I grabbed the rings off her fingers and went out to the backdoor, where I handed the whole lot of jewels and money I'd taken from her purse, to Lorenzo. I then pulled the gloves off and dropped them as I started to run.

"Best split up lads, go our separate ways, get back to the station then you two go onto Crewe. I'll meet you in Leeds tomorrow."

…………

So, yes, even though Leslie had no memory of it, he was in fact there.

…………..

195

An undated and anonymous letter was sent to Green from Spring House, Biddulph Moor, Stoke-on-Trent. It read:

"Dear Lesley,
I have certain reasons to believe that it was not your own will that you murdered Mrs Wilshaw and because of this, I ask you one question. I have all the needed evidence to stop you hanging except one thing. Did your girlfriend really make you love her or was her love ingenuine? (sic). If you answer "Yes", I have enough facts to check this answer. If you answer "No", I have more."

I didn't know what to make of this. Who could have sent it? What answer did he want, that I loved Nora or not. What should I answer 'Yes' to? It just didn't make sense. I wasn't allowed to reply anyway, as the police had opened it beforehand and just showed it to me before taking it away.

As it happens, on further investigation by the police, this letter was signed 'Ten of Club' and turned out to have been written by a 10-year-old boy, living in Spring House, who had no grounds whatsoever for his assertions!

Chapter 25

On 23 December 1952, the day of the execution, only a handful of people stood outside Winson Green Prison at 9am, most of them school children on their Christmas holidays, while a few yards away, Albert Pierrepoint and Syd Dernley were carrying out the sentence of the law and Leslie Green fell 6ft 8in to his death. At no stage had Green shown any signs of remorse and he took to his grave the whereabouts of the missing £2,750 worth of jewellery.

After the execution at Winson Green Prison on the day before Christmas Even, Dernley and the senior hangman, Albert Pierepoint ate a hearty breakfast before returning to take down the body.

Shortly afterwards, a letter was received by the prison governor from Green's widow, Constance, asking for her husband's property to be sent to her. Green had requested that all his property should be sent to Nora Lammey, who later went to live in Golders Green, London, but Green had failed to put this request in writing and the governor was instructed to release what little Green had left, including a Rolls Razor, a Ronson lighter and two wrist watches, to his wife.

Yorkshire Evening Post Wednesday, 31 December 1952
Green case echo in reward offer

Insurance assessors, who are expected to meet senior Staffordshire police officials and members of the family of Mrs Wilshaw, who was found murdered in her villa home at Barlaston on July 16, will probably offer a reward in the region of £200 to 250 for recovery of the balance of the missing jewellery.

Articles valued at between £2,000 and £2,500 are still untraced.

Places where a special watch was being kept were Leeds, Torquay, Birmingham, London and Shrewsbury.

Staffordshire Advertiser, Friday, 12 December 1952
Though the prosecution's case against Leslie Green was based entirely on circumstantial evidence, it took a jury of 10men and two women at the Staffs. Assizes, on Friday, less than half an hour to reject his repeated pleads of innocence, and send him to the condemned cell at Birmingham Prison.

The five-day trial, in which Green admitted himself to be a petty thief, liar, attempted bigamist and poseur, concluded with a 3 hour summing up by Mr Justice Stable after Green's counsel, Mr G G Baker QC, had described the murder as of "unparalleled brutality."

When the file was opened under the Freedom of Information Act, having been embargoed since 1952, the photographs taken at the scene of the murder and the atrocious wounds Mrs Wiltshaw had received, which Judge Stable refused to show the jury, were absent from the file.

Clumsy mistakes and a bad memory, which tripped him up in his lies when cross-examined, cost Green his life and closed the dossier of a crime which initially left barely any clues behind.

Probably the biggest mistake in Green's story was his account of how he came to be seen in possession of two valuable rings, part of £3,000 jewellery missing from the Wiltshaw home, within six hours of the woman's murder.

Another fatal error of Green's revealed in cross examination, was telling a nurse in Leeds that his "aunt" had been murdered with an "old-fashioned poker."

They said two billets of wood, a hammer and a poker had been found in the house and that the police believed Mrs Wiltshaw might have attempted to defend herself with the poker.

An RAF rain-coat was stolen from the murder house. It was found on a train, which Green was alleged to have caught at Stafford on the night of the crime. Its right sleeve was blood-stained.

When Green was seen at Longton, he had a cut on his wrist. His blood and that on the coat were both Group O.

Faced with evidence from the manager of the Station Hotel, Mr Geoffrey Lionel Farr, that he had been seen at the hotel with a blue coat, Green's answer was that the witness was mistaken.

He claimed to have caught an earlier train than the one on which the coat was found. A ticket collector, who gave evidence that he spoke to Green at 7.20pm – nearly 15 minutes after that train's departure, was also mistaken, said Green, although the Station Hotel manager said Green would miss the 7.07pm train if he was staying for dinner, but would be in time for the 7.50pm train.

Piece by piece:
And so the case against him was built up piece by piece. The judge told the jury in his summing up that, if they were satisfied

199

that Green had been seen with the telling rings on the night of the murder, then it pointed that he was both the thief and the murderer. They were to ignore that he admitted lying and that he had a police record and prison sentences.

Several questions are unanswered. One, what happened to the rest of the jewellery? Another, how did Green travel to and from Stafford and Barlaston in the time when he was last seen at the Station Hotel at about 3.30pm and when he was next seen at about 6.30pm.

A question asked by Mr Baker was how Green could possibly have committed the crime and returned to Stafford unruffled and unstained from a murder in which Mrs Wiltshaw had been pulped.

....

Cuthbert Wiltshaw, unable to stand the atmosphere in the house where his beloved Alice Maud had been so cruelly killed, sold it almost immediately and it is now part of the Wedgwood Memorial College. From what I hear from a Stanley Taylor, Cuthbert Wiltshaw had to sell the house off cheaply as no-one wanted to buy it because of the gruesome murder.

Less than two minutes' walk away, the tiny railway station of Barlaston still stands, lonely and so convenient on that day in 1952, when Lesley Green extracted a terrible revenge for his dismissal. A few yards further down the road, the Plume of Feathers public house, now somewhat altered and enlarged, stands by the Trent & Mersey Canal, where the unfortunate Christina Collins feared for her life 113 years earlier (but that's another story).

Mr Wiltshaw moved to Macclesfield. He died in July 1966, aged 73. Constance, Green's wife, remarried and moved away.

Chapter 26

Syd Dernley was a retired colliery worker from Mansfield. In his four years as an assistance executioner, Dernley attended 25 hangings, though he never actually pushed the lever, and the judicial killing of Leslie Green was his last job.

Syd Dernley and his collaborator, journalist David Newman, have taken advantage of a change in the laws on official secrecy to give the first details account of what happened in the execution chamber before hanging was abolished in 1965.

According to Dernley, Green said nothing and didn't struggle as he was strapped up and led to the scaffold.

"At the speed that we hanged him, he would have had the greatest difficulty saying anything at all, even if he'd a mind to."

Contrary to reports, he says, there were no detective standing by the gallows, hoping that Green might make a last-minute statement regarding the missing jewellery stolen from the large house at Barlaston,

Dernley explains in his book "The Hangman's Tale, Memoirs of a Public Executioner", that he and Pierrepoint were shown the police photographs of Mrs Wiltshaw, which bore out the view of an eminent Home Hoffice pathologist that Green was the most vicious murderer of the century.

He acknowledges that hanging might have been a grisly business in the old days, but claims that when he was involved it had reached such a degree of perfection that it could be described as a merciful method of despatch.

Albert Pierrepoint was born in Clayton in the West Riding of Yorkshire. He executed between 425 and 600 people in a 25-year career that ended in 1956. His father Henry and Uncle Thomas were official hangmen before him.

Final Chapter

There was report in the Independent on 12 April 1993 that police were going to re-open an inquiry into the death of Alice Wiltshaw, 62, of Barlaston, Staffordshire, 40 years after Leslie Green, 29, a handyman, was hanged for her murder, which he had denied.

New information suggested three other men were involved in strangling Mrs Wiltshaw in 1952.

(Also, in Hansard – HC Deb 22 April 1993 vol 223 c 180W)

The Evening Sentinel, Thursday, April 22, 1993

A death-bed confession by an underworld informant is believed to have led to a murder inquiry being re-opened.

Information about the killing, 41 years ago, of Mrs Alice Wiltshaw, 62, was given by the informant to a friend.

It was then passed onto senior detectives at Staffordshire Police force headquarters.

The confession is believed to relate to a number of people involved in the murder of Mrs Wiltshaw, wife of a wealthy pottery boss.

Her former chauffeur, Leslie Green, 29, of Blurton, was hanged after being convicted of murder following a five-day trial in Stafford.

Mrs Wiltshaw's blood-soaked body was found at her home in Station Road, Barlaston in July 1952.

She had been bludgeoned around the head with an array of weapons in what was described at the time as "The most vicious murder of the century".

The new information is still being studied by detectives in Staffordshire.

A spokesman said: "Inquiries are still in hand to trace and interview the alleged source of information, which comes from an indirect source.

"Following on from those inquiries any information gained will then have to be verified."

Mrs Wiltshaw's murder sparked one of North Staffordshire's biggest-ever manhunts.

Scotland Yard's Detective Superintendent, Reginald Spooner, was drafted in to co-ordinate the operation.

(Author's note: this was a death-bed confession. I wonder if, by the time this investigation got underhand, the confessor had actually died and, therefore, no verification of any such confession could be made? But, it does ask the question what this confession would have said. We can only surmise – could it have possibly been Lorenzo or Charles? Did they actually exist? If so, what happened to the rest of the jewellery? We will never know.)

The Evening Sentinel, Friday, April 23, 1993 (Rob Cotterill)

MP Chris Mullen, MP for Sunderland, called on Mr Clarke, Home Secretary, to launch a fresh probe into the brutal killing of wealthy pottery boss's wife, Alice Wiltshaw, at her home in Station Road, Barlaston in July 1952. Mr Mullin asked the Secretary of State for the Home Department what steps are being taken to re-open the case of Leslie Green, hanged for the murder of Alice Wiltshaw; and if he will make a statement.

New information believed to relate to the number of people involved in the murder – emerged just over a week ago.

The new information relating to the Leslie Green murder – believed to have come from an underworld informant is being studied by Staffordshire detectives at police headquarters. It is believed to refer to a number of people involved in Mrs Wiltshaw's death.

Inquiries are underway in a bid to trace the source of the information and verify the details passed to detectives.

But, today, Mr Robbins, of Gallowstreet Lane, Newcastle, claimed there was no foundation for the new information.

He said, "There is no evidence of any other person or persons being involved.

They can go ahead and hold an inquiry, but I do not think for one moment it will change history.

The evidence against Leslie Green was overwhelming. When he was arrested, the shoes in his possession matched footprints found at the scene.

The murderer wore a pair of gloves and a hole in them corresponded exactly to a cut on Green's thumb.

Mr Wiltshaw's grey RAF coat was stolen and Green was seen carrying it after the murder. Blood on the coat matched that on the gloves.

He was convicted on overwhelming circumstantial evidence and he knew it.

If he had been innocent he would have appealed against his conviction. He had everything to gain and nothing to lose. He knew he was the person responsible."

In a written reply to the House of Commons yesterday, Home Office Minister of State, Michael Jack, rejected the MP's demand.

In Mr Jack's reply he stated: Mr Green was convicted of the murder of Mrs Wiltshaw on 5 December 1952. The jury made no recommendation as to mercy, and no appeal was lodged. There is no trace of any recent representations having been made to the Home Office concerning the safety of Mr Green's conviction, and neither has any new evidence been presented to us which might bear on the matter. Accordingly, there are no current grounds for re-opening the case.

....

Mr Robbins' involvement in the murder inquiry was appreciated by Mr Wiltshaw, who gave him a Carlton vase in recognition of his hard work.

He was also allowed to keep the brass bowl that was used in the murder of Mrs Wiltshaw!

David Bell 1996 70-79: The ghost of what may have been Maud Alice Wiltshaw was seen in Station Road in the 1970s (info given to Tim Cockin by local author Bruce Braithwaite. Others visiting, including a June Goodwin, have been shocked at seeing what they say are the blood stains at the base of the marble stairs some years after the murder. Mary Mae Lewis has stated to the author that, when she visited on a course there, some years later, there were brown stains, presumably remnants of the blood, on the parquet flooring around the fireplace in the hall.

Acknowledgements

Yorkshire Post and Leeds Mercury
The Yorkshire Evening Post
Staffordshire Advertiser
Stoke Sentinel
Evening Sentinel
Evening Sentinel, FridayApril 23, 1993
The Yorkshire Post and Leeds Intelligencer
The People, Sunday, May 10, 1970
The People world exclusive by Ernest Millen – ex deputy Assitant Commissioner
Evening Sentinel, Friday April 23, 1993
The Guardian 13 September 1952
Staffordshire Advertiser, Friday 18 July 1952
Hanged at Birmingham – Steve Fielding
More Memories of Barlaston by Ernest J Hawkins
The Barlaston Murderer
A Hangman's Tale – Memoirs of a Public Executioner
Staffordshire Murder Stories –David J A Bell
Staffordshire Murders by Alan Hayhurst
Carlton Ware World
Assistance of Tim Cockin and Steve Howe

Other historical novels by the author:
Series:

Footsteps in the Past- ISBN 978-0-244-25919-8 This is history turned into a gripping novel. All historical facts are true.

Jane finds herself whisked back in time to 1842, after seeing a ghostly figure running away from the Ash Hall nursing home where she works.

She finds herself working for Job Meigh, the entrepreneur pottery master who built Ash Hall. He was a violent Victorian, but a great philanthropist and a magistrate. He, and industrialist pottery and mine owners had grown rich from the labours of their workers, who were driven to starvation when their pay was repeatedly cut. The Chartists wanted to get the People's Charter approved by Parliament to offer the people representation in Parliament and the vote. This was rejected, resulting in the violent Pottery Riots.

Jane has to discover why she has been sent back into the past and how to get back, and gets involved with the riots – which lead her into life- threatening danger. She also has to find out who the ghostly figure was.

Footsteps in the Past – The Secret – ISBN 978-0-355-63374-2 The Secret takes the main characters 39 years on from the Pottery Riots of 1842. There is a mining disaster in Bucknall, Stoke, in which Jane and John's son is involved. While nursing John back to health, after his attempt to rescue their son, Jane reminisces what has happened since they met.

Her stories unravel while desperately awaiting news if their son is still alive or not. All historical facts are true.

Footsteps in the Past – John's Story –
ISBN 978-1-716-16818-127
This tells John's story from his youth in the countryside village of Hanley in the 1820s through its industrialisation. It tells John's poignant story of his life, loves and losses in the background of the traumatic times and struggles of people fighting for their rights, representation in Parliament and the vote, which lead to the Pottery Riots of 1842. It also tells of the Cholera Pandemic of 1832 similar to Covid today) and his time in the workhouse.

Munford-Gunn – ISBN 97985-322-313-68

This is a dramatic and thrilling true adventure story following two families of pioneers trying to get to Utah, America to escape prejudice for their beliefs. They meet other prejudice along the way, this time against Africans and First Nation Indians. The book is based on true-life reports.

The families make the life-threatening journey by sailing ship (taking six weeks in those days to cross the Atlantic) then join ox-drawn wagon trains, walking beside these across the 1,300 miles of searing hot plains, dragging the wagons through rivers and perilously hauling them up and over the mountains to get to Salt Lake City. Many die along the way of starvation, dehydration and disease.

The two families meet up. Ann Munford marries George Gunn, only to have to set out immediately to clear land and build settlements – that is until the Black Hawk Wars start.

Review: "What a nightmare. I had to keep reminding myself to breathe. Going to make a cup of tea to get over the trauma. The description is brilliant. I felt I was right there with them."

Printed in Great Britain
by Amazon

70936572R00122